MW00790626

VIKING ADVENTU AMERICA CENTURIES BEFORE COLUMBUS

VIKING WARLORD MAGNUS SAILS ALONG THE NIAGARA RIVER AND REACHES NIAGARA FALLS. ALONG THE WAY, HE FORGES AN ALLIANCE WITH ONE INDIAN TRIBE, BUT HAS TO BATTLE ANOTHER.

Praise for Beyond Vinland

i

"In Magnus Saga Beyond Vineland, John Miles introduces the reader to the gritty world of the Vikings. Using exceptional historical detail Miles is able to give insight about what day-to-day life for the Viking may have been like. This novel is both entertaining as well as informational and will be an entertaining read for fans of historical fiction."—*Matt Steinmetz, MLIS, Librarian and Patron Training and Technology Coordinator in South Carolina*

"John Miles and I served together at both the State University of New York Maritime College and then later in the New York State Naval Militia. His research and writing reveals an exciting Viking adventure. John weaves his own New York State military experience with Magnus' exploration of the Niagara River Valley. This read will resonate with all who embark on its journey"—*Dr. Robert L. Wolf, Major General New York Naval Militia (Ret.)*

Excerpt

The Drakkar long-ships beached themselves next to the village and Magnus along with some Vikingars as security, got out. As they prepared to leave the lakeside, Magnus was surprised to see a Skraeling jogging towards them calling to them in Old Norse. As the man drew nearer, Magnus saw that while he was wearing the buckskin that most Skraelings wore, his features were European. Once he reached the party, he greeted them in Old Norse by saying, "Heill Vikingars, how goes your journey?" Magnus appraised the man and noted that he was of medium height with a red head and a beard that was turning to gray and was probably in his late forties.

After sizing him up, Magnus said, "You are the most Norse looking Skraeling I've ever met." The man laughed and replied, "Yes, I am Olav of the Icelandic Skraelings."

"Olav, how'd you come to be here from Iceland?"

Magnus' Saga Beyond Vinland

John Miles

Moonshine Cove Publishing, LLC

Abbeville, South Carolina U.S.A.

First Moonshine Cove edition January 2021

ISBN: 9781952439018

Library of Congress PCN: 2020925221

Acknowledgment

I could not have written this book without the untiring support of my family. For more than a decade my wife Susanne had the most difficult job in the United States Marine Corps, being the spouse of a Marine. She had to put up with my long hours, frequent lengthy deployments, and my occasionally abrasive personality, an unfortunate result from being in combat. She bore all with amazing equanimity while having to be the primary caregiver for our two very energetic boys. My wife and sons are certainly the biggest blessings in my life, and I thank God for them.

The genesis of this story came from two influential organizations in my life, Texas A&M University and the Marine Corps. I majored in Anthropology and minored in History at Texas A&M, which stoked my interest in other cultures and their histories. Boarding ships with the Marine Corps deploying around the world, I could not help but think this is how the Vikings must have felt a thousand years ago.

One of those operations took me to the land of the Vikings, Norway. Sleeping outdoors there in the winter, I identified with the wanderlust displayed by the Vikings. Journeying somewhere with milder winters, must surely have been an inducement to travel!

Writers of historical fiction cannot write well without access to historical information. I used multiple sources for this book, but some of the most heavily referenced were the websites Academia.edu, ancient-origins.net, pastfactory.com, and the vikinganswerlady.com. I must also thank my publisher Gene D. Robinson at Moonshine Cove LLC. Before this novel was published, I had never written a book. My background as an author was in writing magazine articles.

The skillsets needed in those two writing styles differ significantly. Gene took a chance on an unproven novelist and walked me through the process to completion. A sincere thanks to you and your team Gene!.

About the Author

John Miles is a retired United States Marine Corps Lieutenant Colonel and former college professor who now writes and delivers lectures about historical topics to groups. He has presented lectures to multiple Scottish Highland Games, Celtic Festivals, and military units throughout the Southeast. In addition to highland games and military organizations, he also gives historical presentations at various retirement homes and libraries in the Carolinas.

In addition to his novel *Magnus' Saga - Beyond Vinland*, John is a multiple-time published author in *Marine Corps Gazette*, the professional journal of the Marine Corps. Furthermore, he also writes articles for periodicals that cover history and has been published numerous times. These magazines include *American Frontiersman, The Highlander, Military History, Ireland's Own,* and *Scotland Magazine.*

He holds or has held membership in the following organizations: Clan Gillean USA, Clan Donnachaidh USA, The Scottish American Military Society (SAMS), Scottish American Society Palm Beach, FL, the St. Andrew's Society of Albany, NY, and the Scottish American Society of Tidewater, VA.

He received his Master of Arts degree in Military Studies from American Military University and his Batchelor of Arts degree in Anthropology with a minor in History from Texas A&M University.

www.historicallectures.com

Chapter One

Magnus took the object from the leather bag it was kept in whenever he was at sea. As Magnus was a healthy, well-built man hailing from the Vik, he was at sea more often than not, it seemed. The Vik was the name of a bay between the lands of the Varangians, or Rus, to the east, and the lands of the Norsemen to the west. The people that came from the region were known as Vikingars. When a Vikingar sailed on a long ship for a voyage of trade, exploration or raid, it was known as going on a Viking. And Magnus the Vikingar was certainly going on a Viking now. A very, very long Viking.

The object he took from the waterproofed leather bag was known as a sun stone. The sunstone was a clear calcite crystal, called Icelandic spar, mined in Scandinavia. The stones were used to guide the Norsemen by revealing the position of the sun even when it was obscured by cloud or had recently sunk beneath the horizon. And in the north Atlantic, it was frequently overcast. Over time, the Vikings had learned that by covering the crystal with an opaque sheet that had a hole in the center, the calcite worked particularly well in pinpointing the position of the sun. As every Vikingar worth his salt knew, so long as you knew roughly what time of day it was, and you knew where the sun was in the sky, you knew what direction you're traveling. The sunstone even worked after the sun set and went down beyond the horizon. It wasn't until the moon came up and the stars came out, that the sunstone failed to find the sun. Magnus had talked with Vikingars who had travelled the silk road very far to the east. They had mentioned that the peoples there used what they called a magnetic compass. It had a needle that always pointed north. Magnus thought that possessing one of those would help tremendously with cloudy night-time travel. If the sky was clear and the stars were out, all Norsemen knew where to sail. So long as one could see the constellation Óðins vagn, or the god Odin's Wagon, he knew exactly where north was. If it was overcast, then navigation at nighttime was difficult, and the ship's captain had to try and read currents in the sea or watch for sea birds flying by. A good captain could usually get a general idea of his direction of sail on an overcast night, but one of those eastern compasses would make life much easier. Some of the Vikingars who had travelled far to the east had endeavored to trade for one to bring home, but they were very valuable, and none had succeeded yet. Magnus knew that it was just a matter of time before magnetic compasses arrived in Europe, and that would make going on a Viking that much easier.

Magnus was named for a distant ancestor that had been a King of Norway. His forefather had done much to extend the power of the Norse into the land of the Gaels. And the earlier Magnus was the last Norwegian king to have died in battle overseas, there in the land of the Gaels. King Magnus spent so much time with the tribe the Romans called the Scotti, that he took to wearing a kilt. Hence, he was nicknamed Magnus Barelegs. This Magnus, his descendant, was going on the farthest Viking he'd ever undertaken. He was forty years old and had been a

Vikingar since his mid-teens and had become a Jomsviking when he was twenty. The Jomsvikings were mercenaries that were highly selective in deciding whom to admit to their order. Membership was restricted to men of proven valor between eighteen and fifty. In order to gain admission, prospective members were required to prove themselves with a feat of strength, often taking the form of a ritual duel, or holmgang, with a current Jomsviking. Magnus's feat of strength was somewhat different than the usual holmgang. He was told that there was a bear, that the Vikings called a bjørn, whose recent hibernation den was up the mountain near a local village. This bjørn was well known for killing the villagers' cattle and sheep; and killing a bear in one-on-one combat should certainly qualify Magnus for admission into the Jomsvikings.

More times than he could remember, Magnus had retold the saga of how he was able to best a ferocious animal easily four times his size. Magnus had armed himself with a stout spear and a Sparth or Dane battle-axe almost four feet long. He used several Elkhund hunting dogs to track the bjørn to its den. Magnus had no doubt that they had found the bear's den when they commenced an ear-splitting barking, growling and howling. Magnus had been concerned that the bjørn would remain in its cave and force him to enter the confined space to fight it. He needn't have worried, as the dogs let out such a hellacious racket, no living creature could have slept through it.

The bear didn't appear to relish the rude manner in which it was awoken from its winter slumber. It came out of its den growling and showing its teeth. Magnus, who was standing outside the entrance to the cave, wasted no time with formalities. He thrust his stout spear deep into the bjørn's chest. Such a thrust would have dropped any man immediately, with the possible exception of a Berserker. Berserk warriors fought in such a trance like fury, that you often had to cleave their heads with an axe to stop them. If you didn't, you would have to wait until they bled to death from their other wounds. However, while they were bleeding out, they would still be killing all the opposing warriors they could.

After taking Magnus's spear thrust in its chest, the bear didn't drop dead. Instead, it let out a growl that even drowned out the Elkhunds' howling, swept one of its forepaws down on the shaft of the spear, and broke it. Magnus now dropped his useless spear haft and grabbed the sparth axe in both hands. He was now very glad he had brought the Elkhunds. The dogs, whose appearance and aggressive behavior were not very far removed from the wolves they descended from, now launched on the bear. A fifty-pound dog attacking an almost thousand-pound bear may seem foolhardy for the dog, but when a pack of several of those near wolves' attack in unison, one almost pities the bjørn. The dogs began jumping up and biting the bear from all different angles. When the bear would turn to face the dog biting it, the other dogs would then bite the bear from another point. While this was occurring, Magnus swung his Dane axe with all might on the bear, trying to avoid hitting an Elkhund. The dogs were usually nimble and coordinated enough to avoid the björn's attempts at stopping them, but one of the Elkhunds was a bit too slow and was caught by one of the bear's paw strikes. The unfortunate dog was knocked several feet into the air, and the bear's almost four-inch-long claws inflicted wounds which would prove fatal. However, the loss of one of their comrades didn't deter the rest of the pack at all, and if anything, they fought with even more ferocity.

With the dogs sinking their canines into the bear, and Magnus burying his 8-inch cutting edge axe repeatedly into it, the outcome was inevitable. As blood loss weakened the bear, its valiant struggles grew ever weaker, until Magnus was able to deliver the final coup-de-grace that dispatched it. After the bjorn's death, the remaining dogs then tried to tend to their wounded mate, by licking its wounds. Unfortunately, there was nothing they could do, and after it died, the pack commenced a very melancholy howling. While this transpired, Magnus said a prayer of thanks to Skadi, the Norse Goddess of Winter and of the Hunt.

Now that he had bested the bjorn, Magnus had to bring proof to the Jomsvikings. The only way he could envisage accomplishing that, was to bring back part of the bear. As it would take a fair amount of time to skin the animal, and evening was approaching, Magnus decided to wait till tomorrow for that task. Magnus wished for a moment that this fight had taken place in the summer, when the sun stays up well past midnight. He quickly told himself that this thought was nonsensical, as bjorns don't hibernate in the summer, so locating it, even with the noses of the hunds, would have proved problematic. Since the skinning would have to wait, Magnus decided to use his axe to cut off the dead bear's front paws. He felt certain that when he showed the Jomsvikings these, they would believe that he had in fact killed it in one-on-one combat.

It wasn't a one-on-one fight as the Elkhunds had proved invaluable. If it hadn't been for their noses, Magnus probably would have never found the bear's den. If it hadn't been for their incessant barking and howling, he probably wouldn't have been able to draw the bear out of its den to fight. As brave as he was, Magnus shuddered at the thought of having to enter the bear's den to face it. Finally, if it hadn't been for the dogs' constant assault on the bear, Magnus knew he would have had a hard fight to get clear of here. Regardless of the hunds' invaluable assistance, Magnus was the only Vikingar in the fight, and that was what the Jomsvikings were looking for.

After hacking off the bear's forepaws, Magnus made sure he noted landmarks so could find his way back tomorrow to skin the animal. Skinning an animal that large would prove tiresome, but he knew it was well worth it. The reason was the Berserkers would pay handsomely for a bear skin. The Old Norse words ber-serkr meant a "bear-shirt" or "bear coat". In battle, the berserkers would wear bearskin coats, and were subject to fits of frenzy. They would howl like wild beasts, foam at the mouth, and gnaw the iron rim of their shields. According to belief, during these fits they were immune to steel and made great havoc in the ranks of the enemy. To "go berserk" translates as " to change form," and in this case, to "enter a state of wild fury." In a berserker's mind, he was literally able to shape-shift into a bear. And after wearing the bearskin in battles, the body of a dead berserker was laid out in it prior to his funeral rites. For these reasons, bearskin coats were highly sought after by berserker cults and considered very valuable. So, not only would killing the bear gain Magnus admission into the Jomsvikings, but its hide would also earn him a pretty penny.

Magnus chuckled to himself as he remembered displaying the bear paws to the admission council of the Jomsvikings. To say these hardened warriors were impressed, would be an understatement. One of them stated that he was glad Magnus hadn't chosen to partake in a ritualistic duel or Holmgang. Holmgangs involved two warriors being confined in a small space hacking at each other with swords. Each combatant was permitted a certain number of shields, and when one shield was splintered, grabbed another. Holmgangs were usually fought until first blood was drawn, or one of the opponents was out of shields. In extreme cases, if the duelists had agreed to it beforehand, it was decided by death. Even if death hadn't been agreed to, combatants often received fatal wounds from the sword blows. For entrance into the Jomsvikings, the holmgang was never intended to be fatal, as that would be very costly in mercenaries. As the impressed high-ranking Jomsviking stated, if Magnus could kill a bear in a duel, he wouldn't envy the Jomsviking selected to fight him in a holmgang. As Magnus had thought, the bear paws earned him admission into the Jomsvikings and he had lived that life for over a decade.

Once admitted, the Jomsvikings required adherence to a strict code of conduct in order to instill a sense of military discipline amongst its members. Any significant violation of these rules was frequently punished with immediate expulsion from the order. Each Jomsviking was bound to defend his brothers, as well as to avenge their deaths in battle. Magnus learned that it was forbidden to speak ill of his fellows or to quarrel with them. If a feud between members arose, it would be mediated by Jomsviking officers. Jomsvikings were forbidden to show fear or to flee in the face of an enemy of equal or inferior strength. However, Jomsviking officers could order an orderly retreat in the face of vastly outnumbering forces. All spoils of battle were to be equally distributed among the entire brotherhood. No Jomsviking was permitted to be absent from their base for more than three days without the permission of the brotherhood. No women or children were allowed within the fortress walls, and none were to be taken captive. This was because the officers knew that where women were, would also be lust and jealousies for them amongst the Jomsvikings. A Jomsviking could get married, with his commander's authorization, but the wife and any children would have to live outside the fortress. The Jomsvikings were not loyal to any king or principality and would fight for any lord able to pay their substantial fees. Their stronghold Jomsborg was located on the southern shore of the Baltic Sea, and the ranks contained Norsemen, Danes, Rus, and even Ice-Landers. Magnus served as a Jomsviking mercenary for a decade throughout Europe. He learned a tremendous amount about himself and his comrades during that time, and overall, enjoyed his service. It was also financially rewarding, otherwise no one would risk becoming a mercenary. However, the kings and princes in Scandinavia grew tired of a mercenary army in their midst and began taking available opportunities to curtail the Jomsvikings' strength and reach. Magnus and his comrades could see that the

Jomsvikings' power was waning, so Magnus decided to take his battle winnings and leave the order.

With his accumulated wealth, Magnus was able to purchase a farmstead, some cattle and sheep to fill it, and some slaves to work it. Slavery was very prevalent in Viking age Scandinavia and Magnus estimated that 2 of every 10 people were enthrall. A thrall was the Old Norse word for a slave, and to be enthralled was to be under someone else's control. The earliest thralls had been taken in Viking raids on other Vikingar villages. Eventually, as the Viking raids started going offshore to other parts of Europe, the slaves came from there. At the present time, most of the thralls were coming from the islands of the Anglo-Saxons and Gaels.

Magnus remembered the first Viking that he had gone on there. The Viking long ships had landed in a protected bay, that he was told the local Gaels called Dubh-Linn, or a pool of dark water. They were not the first Vikings to land there, and Dublin would be under Viking control for years. As previous Viking raiders had taken anything of value, including slaves, from the area around Dublin, Magnus and his comrades purchased provisions from the Viking traders there, and set out. They sailed up the coast until they heard of a village that appeared to be relatively untouched, that was quite a way up a river leading to the coast. Fortunately, the draught of their longships were no more than four feet, so they could sail and row very far up rivers. And because of their relatively light construction and large crews of up to sixty or eighty, if the river got too shallow or had obstructions, the Vikingars could haul it on to land and man-handle it until it could be put back in.

This fact was to the detriment of numerous European riverside villages, that were many miles from the coast.

Magnus's raiding party proceeded up-river until they reached the targeted village and then beached their ships on the riverbank. The villagers had seen their approach, and in a panic had all gathered at the local kirk, where they worshipped their God, called Christ. To them this was holy ground, and as it was sacred, no Christian would dare commit violence there. However, while Christianity was making significant inroads into Viking Scandinavia, many Vikingars still worshipped Odin, Thor, and the host of other Norse gods and goddesses. Therefore, to the still pagan Vikingars, a kirk was just a building that the villagers fled to when threatened. It was also a building that contained the majority of the town's treasure. If a man had monetary wealth, he had two options. He could either hide it under his bed, and hope he wasn't robbed, or give it to the local church to watch. Since that was Holy Ground, it was safe there, unless Vikingars attacked of course. Magnus had been told that in return for watching a man's gold and silver, the church would receive a tithe, worth ten percent of the accumulated wealth. Magnus wondered if after a Viking raid sacked a church or monastery and took the wealth stored there, if the clergy then returned the various tithes to the now destitute villagers. Seeing that the villagers had all conveniently gathered themselves together to be plundered, the Vikingars proceeded to do just that.

Magnus did have to give the Gaels credit for their fighting ability, even though they were clearly outmatched by the Viking raiders. Magnus clearly remembered one red-headed Gael wielding a type of axe, Magnus was afterwards told was called a Celt. The Vikingars used battle axes known as Sparth or Dane axes. The Irish Celt axe was somewhat different. The Viking axes were heavy which required it to be used with both hands. The Gaelic axe was smaller and more finely wrought. And the Gaels only used one hand to wield the Celt axe. The warrior would place his thumb along the handle to guide the blow. And guide it very effectively did he. This Gael was obviously a warrior, as in addition to the Celt axe, he had a shield and wore a type of armor. The shield was oval shaped, made of wicker covered in leather and convex on the outside. The armor was a primitive corselet made of bull-hide and stitched with iron thongs. On his head he wore a cap made of hard tanned leather, reinforced with iron and bronze bars and painted a bright red. The Gael's armor may have seemed primitive to some of the wealthy Vikingars, who wore chainmail and iron helmets. In reality, it wasn't much different than the lamellar armor worn by many of the other Vikings, as well as the types of various foreign armor worn by those that had captured it in raids or traded for. The Gael and two of his comrades, who were similarly equipped, formed a back-to-back triangle inside the entranceway of the kirk. As the Vikings battered down the door to gain entrance, the Irishmen were waiting. Since the stone vestibule limited maneuverability, the Vikings couldn't assault the Gaels in a Svinfylking, or flying wedge formation. Instead, the Vikings had to come at them with no more than two or three abreast. The big red head, who was almost as tall as Magnus, at six feet, stood a head taller than his comrades.

He must have been a leader of some importance, as the other two clearly followed him. He positioned himself facing the door, so the Vikings would have to face him first, upon entry into the kirk.

The effectiveness of the Irishman's bull-hide armor now showed its value. The Vikings initially attempted to use their weapon with the most range, their spears. Two Vikings who possessed good throwing arms, paired up using their spears as javelins at the start of the melee. They both threw their spears simultaneously at the three Celtic warriors. The big redhead caught one spear on his shield, and while the other spear hit him in the side, his bull-hide armor apparently absorbed the blow, as the Irishman appeared to suffer no serious ill effects from it. Since those two Vikingars were now without their spears for the remainder of the skirmish, none of the rest chanced throwing theirs. Another Vikingar did use his spear as a thrusting weapon, but the Gael again proved his ability as a warrior. Seeing the spear armed Vikingar approaching, the Gael inexplicably turned his body to the right exposing his left flank to the spear thrust. Some of the seasoned veterans recognized this defensive move at once, but the young Vikingar with the spear did not, and did exactly what the Gael expected. The Viking thrust his spear with all his might at the Gael's left side, and in mid-thrust the Irishman swung his shield around to the left knocking the spear aside. The Vikingar was now off balance and the Gael demonstrated his adroitness with his Celt axe. Aiming the head of the axe with his right thumb, the Irishman buried it in the unarmored neck of the Vikingar. As Magnus watched this transpire, the thought he had was "and so the Valkyries are now taking another Vikingar to Odin's Valhalla." First blood to the Gaels, but there would be plenty more spilt this day.

Fully understanding that warfare was something these three Gaels understood, the Vikingars pulled back to adjust their plan of attack. Magnus thought up a plan that might work. He would be on the right, and Einar on the left. Magnus would go in first, using his Dane axe to distract the Gael, allowing Einar to finish him off. After telling the others of the plan, a young Vikingar named Brandt asked Magnus if he could take his place. He explained that Magnus, as a Jomsviking, had nothing to prove. Whereas Brandt, being a relatively inexperienced Vikingar, needed to establish his credentials as a warrior. Magnus thought briefly about it and then agreed. So, it was to be Brandt and Einar that tackled the big Irishman. Brandt came at the Irishman with his Sparth axe raised as if to strike, and as expected, the Gael raised his shield to block it. Instead of swinging the axe, Brandt hooked the curved horn of his axe head over the edge of the Irishman's shield, pulling it down. Einar who had made as if to attack the Gael to the side of the big redhead, then instead thrust his sword into the now unprotected side of the Irish warrior. The man's bull-hide armor still did its job of absorbing most of the blow, but the momentum of the thrust pushed the Gael off balance. Brandt was waiting for this very event and now released his axe and took the sword held in his left hand to stab the man in the throat. The big Irishman was now dead, but Einar didn't have long to celebrate, as the Gael that he had feigned an attack on, now swung his Celt axe down on Einar's outstretched left hand, severing it. Brandt then picked up his Dane axe and clove that Irishman's head from his shoulders, which left Brandt exposed to the final Gael's sword, which entered Brandt's unarmored armpit and thence his heart and lungs. The remaining Gael was then dispatched by the other Vikingars. The three Celtic warriors had given a good account of themselves and had killed two Viking raiders and cleaved off the hand of another before dying.

Afterwards, the Vikings tied a tourniquet around Einar's left arm. He was a brave lad, and told everyone that after his wound healed up, he could still go a Viking as he could strap his shield on his left arm and still use his sword with his right. Everyone respected his grit and determination but realized that if he didn't succumb to a fatal blood infection, very few Viking warlords would be willing to take a one-handed Vikingar on a raid. And this didn't bode well for Einar's future. Although his father, Thorkell the Tall, had been a relatively well-to-do merchant when he recently died, Einar had inherited none of the wealth. The reason being that Viking society practiced both polygamy and primogeniture. A Viking could have as many wives as he could afford. And being a reasonably successful merchant, Einar's father could afford several. He had ended up with five wives, whose ages ranged between forty-five and twenty-five when he died. As the Vikings practiced primogeniture as well, only the oldest son from the first wife, inherited anything when the father died. Unfortunately for Einar, not only was he not the eldest son from the first wife, but he also didn't have a good relationship with Valdr, who was. Valdr, which meant 'ruler' in old Norse, never failed to act like he believed he was. Growing up, he always reminded his siblings that he would inherit everything. Therefore, his relationships with his brethren were strained, to put it mildly. It didn't help that the first wife didn't have good relationships with the other wives or their children.

Astrid, Thorkell's original wife, was never happy when Thorkell decided he needed another wife and didn't hide her displeasure. She was well renowned for her jealousy, and while many Viking women would try to get along with their husband's fellow wives, she would not. She often went out of her way to let the other wives know that they were secondary to her, and on the nights that Thorkell was sleeping with another wife, Astrid would go out of her way to be rude to their children. It should be no surprise that Valdr acted the way he did, with his mother as a role model. With Einar's future as a Vikingar now in doubt, and his eldest brother not willing to do anything to assist him, Magnus worried what would become of the young man.

After the three Gaelic warriors were deceased, the remainder of the villagers offered no more resistance, so the Vikingars prepared to divvy up the loot. The leader of the raid took his share first, and then the others got theirs. The Irish village must have been reasonably wealthy, as there was a good amount of the villager's gold and silver kept at the church. After that was apportioned, the raiders went through the buildings in the village to find anything else of value. And they did. The discovered several young villagers, that their families had hid in stables and hay lofts. The young people were some of the most valuable commodities, as they would fetch the most as thralls. Each raider earned at least one thrall to take back to the Vik. Once there, the thralls would be auctioned off, with the youngest and fittest getting the best prices. Magnus, being a former Jomsviking and one of the most experienced Viking raiders, got a good share of the valuables as well as the thralls. The thralls he received were a strapping young man who would fetch a good price as a farm hand, and an attractive young woman that should fetch a good price as a maid servant. An added bonus was that the young woman spoke rudimentary Norse, which she learned from another woman who was a fellow nun.

The Vikingars loaded their spoils and thralls on their longships as well as plundered provisions for the sea journey back to the Vik. It would take at least a week's sail to get back to the Vik from Ireland, depending on the winds and currents. A week plus with nothing to do but assist in sailing and rowing the longship could be maddingly dull, and usually the time would be spent gambling and telling sea-stories to impress the younger Vikingars. Magnus was glad that the female thrall spoke some Norse, as it would give him someone else to talk to. This conversing would also improve her ability to speak Norse, which would make her even more marketable as a thrall. Magnus imagined the thrall auction, where he would have her say in Norse, "ma'am please have your husband buy me, I can't wait to milk your cows." Magnus knew that selling a healthy young thrall that spoke the language of its eventual master was going to be rewarding for him. The fact that she was also attractive, would make the hours spent speaking with her not tiresome in the least. Magnus asked her what she was called, and she replied Brigid. She explained that Brigid was a highly renowned Saint of the Christian Church in the land of the Gaels.

To make conversation, Magnus asked her what Brigid had done to earn her Sainthood? Brigid relished talking about her namesake and said, that St. Brigid's father was a pagan chieftain, and her mother a Pictish Christian. Brigid was named after the goddess Brigid of her father's religion, the goddess of fire. Magnus interrupted here by saying; "We Vikingars also have gods associated with fire. The god and goddess of fire are Logi, and his wife Glod. They are both fire giants, and I imagine that watching them make love, would be interesting to say the least!"

Now blushing a deep red, Brigid quickly said, "That as a young woman, Brigid left behind her half-pagan roots and converted to Christianity, having been a fan of Saint Patrick's preaching for some time. Her father was not pleased when she felt a longing to enter religious life and tried in vain to keep her at home at first. Stuck in her family house, she became known for her generosity and charity. She never refused any poor beggar who came knocking at her father's door, and the household went through a steady supply of milk, flour, and other essentials she gave away. When a leper came begging one day and having nothing else to hand, she even gave him her father's jeweled sword."

Magnus guffawed so loudly that he had to wipe tears from his eyes before Brigid continued, "Her father finally gave in, and sent Brigid to a convent, possibly just to avoid bankruptcy. Brigid embarked on a career as a convent founder, a place for women wishing to dedicate themselves to serving Christ. However, she is really known for her activity in Kildare, which became her most important life's work. There she founded Kildare Abbey, a monastery for both nuns and monks."

Intrigued at the concept of a convent, Magnus asked more about one's purpose. Brigid said, 'The daily life of nuns was based on the three main vows: The Vow of Poverty, the Vow of Chastity, and the Vow of Obedience. Brigid explained what each vow meant, and Magnus was taken aback by the one concerning chastity. He asked Brigid if that vow ended once the nuns got married. Brigid blushed and said that as nuns considered themselves wed to Jesus, they never married mortal men.

Magnus smiled and said, "Your Jesus must truly be a God, as anyone that could handle that many wives surely must be immortal." Magnus didn't have the heart to tell her that as a thrall, while the vows of poverty and obedience and poverty would certainly still apply, her vow of chastity would not. Magnus felt a twinge of guilt thinking that as an attractive young woman, Brigid's future as a thrall probably included being some rich man's bed slave, or frille. Magnus was not an emotional man, but as he conversed with her, he was growing fond of the former nun Brigid. And the thought of her going from serving her god to becoming a wealthy man's sexual plaything, on account of Magnus's actions, was causing him distress.

To take his mind off her probable future, Magnus asked her what else nuns did at a convent. Brigid stated that, "The life of a nun was dedicated to worship, reading, and working in the convent or nunnery. In addition to their attendance at church, the nuns spent several hours in private prayer, called meditation". She said, "Most women were not usually well educated in the land of the Gaels, but some nuns were taught to read and write Latin, the language of the church. The convents and nunneries provided the only source of education for women in the land, although the knowledge the nuns were provided with was carefully screened by the Church hierarchy. Their daily life was filled with washing and cooking for the monastery, raising the necessary supplies of vegetables and grain, producing wine, ale and honey, providing medical care for the community, educating the novice nuns, spinning, weaving and embroidery and finally illuminating, or drawing artwork, in written manuscripts."

Magnus realized that her background made her the most marketable thrall he'd ever come across. Not only well-to-do farmers, but also wealthy merchants and princes would be interested in purchasing her for a substantial price. For her sake, Magnus wished that she was ugly, so she would be bought solely based on her domestic abilities. Admiring her green eyes, clear skin, reddish hair and very attractive build from across the ship's hull, Magnus knew that whatever wealthy man purchased her, would expect more of a return on his investment. Especially when the prospective buyers were made aware of her previous vow of chastity. A beautiful young woman, well-schooled in domestic chores, who was also a virgin, would earn Magnus a pretty penny.

Reflecting on this, Magnus hoped Brigid's Jesus would forgive him for what would happen to her. Taking a break from asking her questions about being a nun, Magnus asked Brigid what she thought of the Vikingars.

She paused before replying; "Many of the Bishops believe that the arrival of you Vikings was prophesized in the Bible. And one of them preached a sermon on it recently which I well remember."

Magnus was taken aback by this as he waited for her to continue. "The Bishop's sermon was based on the book of Jeremiah, Chapter I, verse 14 reads, '*Out of the north an evil shall break forth upon all the inhabitants of the land.*" And he then recited a new verse introduced into the Litany of the Church, '*From the fury of the Northmen, O Lord, deliver us.*'"

After sailing around the top of the land of the Scotti, Magnus's boat proceeded to cross the North Atlantic back to the land of the Norse. Upon arrival at the village by the fjord that they sailed from, the raiders disembarked and took their spoils and thralls back to their homes. Magnus's wife Esja was overseeing the thralls' work when Magnus arrived at his farmstead. After giving him a long hug and kiss, Esja admired all the loot that Magnus brought home. He explained to her that the male thrall only spoke Gaelic, but as did a couple of the other thralls, he could be put to work immediately. He explained that Brigid spoke rudimentary Norse and elaborated on the domestic skills she possessed.

Over a welcome flagon of mead, Magnus explained Brigid's previous existence as a Nun, and all the vows she had taken. Upon hearing about the vow of chastity, Esja's eyes widened. "A young woman as attractive as her that is still a virgin? Do you realize how much money she'll draw at the thrall auction?"

Magnus nodded his head. "Aye, I do! Did I not tell your father that I would provide you a comfortable life?" Finishing her own mead, Esja grabbed Magnus by the hand and drew him to their bed chamber. "Now let me do my part to make my husband as comfortable as possible."

After they finished, Magnus and Esja continued to discuss the fate of Brigid. Esja said, "You realize that if we let her sleep in the hut with the other thralls, she won't remain a virgin for long."

"Aye, if we billet her there, I doubt she'd be a virgin come tomorrow morning."

"I realize that letting thralls sleep in our longhouse isn't something we've ever done, but in her case, I think it's the best way to protect our investment."

Magnus rubbed his beard and answered, "I agree, it will also give us time to observe her domestic abilities and see if we need to give her more training prior to the auction."

Esja brought Brigid in from the barn where she was milking a goat that they would make cheese from. Remembering that Magnus had said she spoke Norse, Esja introduced herself to her. Fully realizing the position that she was now in, Brigid reacted to Esja as she would to a Mother Superior. She was respectful and did her best to show that she would do everything she could for her new masters. Esja asked Brigid to explain the work she had done at the convent. In her broken Norse, Brigid explained the daily workload of a Nun. After listening and asking for edification of a few tasks, Esja was satisfied.

Looking intently at Brigid, Esja asked, "Do you realize that if we let you sleep in the quarters with the other thralls, your vow of chastity will soon be forfeited?"

Studying her feet, Brigid said, "That is why the church never allows Nuns and Monks to share communal lodging."

"Therefore, you will sleep in a corner of our longhouse, where Magnus and I can help you protect your vow of chastity."

Esja didn't elaborate that the reason they cared about Brigid's virginity was by way of protecting a valuable commodity. Esja reasoned that as Brigid appeared to be an intelligent woman, she'd probably already deduced that anyway. Brigid expressed her appreciation and Esja showed where she would be sleeping. Brigid made her bed and then returned to the other thralls to finish the farm work. After Brigid left the house, Esja spoke with Magnus, "She's a fit girl, given a little time, she might be able to join my shieldmaidens."

"Whoever buys her may not wish to risk her life as a shieldmaiden."

'True, but if the village is attacked and looted, her owner would probably lose his precious thrall anyway."

Magnus grabbed Esja's bottom and said, "Since she is going to be sleeping in here, I'd feel bad if we made love with her in the room."

"You think your sense of decorum would stop us from loving each other?"

Magnus laughed. "Probably not!"

Chapter Two

As Magnus located the suns position in the overcast sky via his sunstone, he reflected on what lead to his current Viking. After leaving the Jomsvikings, Magnus had initially taken time to establish his farmstead near one of the numerous fjords around the Vik. After he purchased the land, he had purchased the thralls to farm it, and the animals to fill it. The first order of business was to construct a hús, or house, to live in. Due to their ship building prowess, the Vikings were excellent carpenters, so building a wooden house was second nature. With the assistance of a few fellow Vikingars, and his thralls, Magnus cleared timber and got a comfortable hús built.

After constructing his abode, Magnus then built the bairn, or barn, for his animals. Scandinavian winters were snowy and cold, and even with the animals' thick fur, having a barn to shelter in on wintry nights would prove beneficial. After clearing the land and building the structures, Magnus was ready to have the thralls begin farming it. The sheep's wool was a valuable commodity in cold Scandinavia, as was the cows' and goats' milk.

Magnus had bought ten thralls total, five females and five males. The males he would use primarily for the timber harvesting business on his land. The females would take care of the house and the farm work, including the gathering of the wool the sheep shed and weaving of it into garments, and the milking of the cows and goats. Some of the female thralls were skilled in the process of cheese making, which would also be a lucrative side business for Magnus. After establishing his farmstead and organizing the working of it, Magnus had one last task to accomplish. He needed to find a wife to help him manage it all.

In the Viking age Scandinavia, marriage was more akin to a business arrangement and family alliance rather than a love-match. For a Vikingar to get a woman to marry him, he had to impress, convince, and pay her family. The prospective bride did have some input on whether she wanted to accept her suitor, unlike in many other contemporary cultures. Regardless, the woman's family would be the deciding factor. Magnus reasoned that the best way to meet some of the eligible young women was to attend a 'thing'.

In the Viking Age, things were the public assemblies of the freemen of a province. They functioned as both parliaments and courts at different levels of society. Their purpose was to solve disputes and make political decisions, and thing sites were also often the place for public religious rites. Only free men of full age could participate in the assembly, and women were present at many things despite being left out of the decision-making bodies. Besides serving a municipal government function, things were also community get togethers where Norsemen would interact with their neighbors. Magnus had attended several things and knew that the local Karls, who were the freemen and landowners, often brought their wedding age daughters to the things. Magnus had even occasionally seen the local Jarls, or Viking Earls, bring their daughters to the things as well. Whether she was the daughter of a

Karl or a Jarl, so long as she was pretty, a hard worker, and could keep him warm on the long winter nights, Magnus couldn't care less.

Marriage was a relatively involved process in Viking society, and freeborn women were viewed as having intrinsic value. Marriage was a contractual arrangement between the families of the bride and groom in the Viking Age, just as it was throughout other areas of medieval Europe. The most sought-after brides by well-to-do families were virgins. An unwed maiden was a marketable commodity who could be used to bring wealth to her family via her bride-price, and to help form favorable alliances with other families when she wed.

Magnus's situation as a bachelor was a little different than the norm. For one, his mother and father were already deceased. Therefore, from Magnus's perspective, the familial alliance component of a marriage was relatively void. Secondly, he really wasn't interested in paying the bride-price for the daughter of a Jarl. Magnus knew that for the foreseeable future he would continue his career of embarking on Vikings. Therefore, he would be gone from his farmstead for long periods. So, his wife would be the one to manage the daily activities of farm life. Magnus doubted that many prim and proper daughters of Jarls would be able to efficiently do that. And this was another reason Magnus was not going to use one of the female thralls he'd purchased as a bed-slave. He knew that if he did, that would create tremendous jealousies amongst his other thralls. Those jealousies would create ill-will, which would in-turn negatively affect their willingness to work. The thralls were slaves that had no say in the work they did. However, from his service as a Jomsviking, Magnus knew that that people labored differently, depending on if they did it because they wanted to, or had to.

Magnus was under no illusions about his thralls' willingness to be his slaves. Yet, he also knew that if he made their lives as bearable as possible, they would count themselves lucky to be his thralls. Therefore, they would still do labor on his farm, even when he was away on a Viking. Especially, if he had a strong, confident wife to provide them guidance. So, what Magnus was seeking was probably the daughter of a local Karl. Due to the wealth he had accumulated over his decade as a Jomsviking, Magnus did not foresee the bride-price being a problem. So, Magnus would attend the upcoming Thing, look for available maidens, and if he found an appealing prospect, begin negotiations with her father or guardian acting as her fastnandi. Once Magnus and the girl's fastnandi agreed on terms, the marriage would transpire.

On the day of the thing, Magnus thought it wise to look as appealing as possible to any potential wives. Therefore, he went to the nearest stream, disrobed and took his weekly bath. Almost all Scandinavians, with the possible exceptions of the 2 in 10 who were thralls, bathed weekly. Magnus remembered going overseas on his first Viking, and after taking some prisoners destined to become thralls, smelling their body odor. Magnus had the translator ask them when the last time was, they'd bathed, and their reply was, never. Apparently, some European cultures did not regularly wash their bodies, as did the Vikingars.

Magnus was not going to spend over two weeks in the small confines of a long ship with the stench of unwashed thralls. So, he had each thrall get a nice, long dunking in the bay where the long ships were beached. Evidently, some European cultures didn't value learning how to swim either. The stinky thralls didn't seem to enjoy their bath time in the least.

After a raid, the Vikingars knew it wise not to delay getting back on their ships and departing. More than one successful Viking raiding party had been slow to leave, to their detriment. After hearing about the sacking of a village, it wasn't unusual for the other local villages to band together and try to catch the Vikingars responsible. If a Viking raiding party was caught on the beach by a numerically larger and very angry village militia, then there would undoubtably be many more Vikingars in Odin's Valhalla that night. So, the raiding party Magnus was on wasted no time loading the ships and rowing out into the bay.

It was only after they were several hundred yards offshore that Magnus caught whiff of the thralls. Not willing to inhale that aroma for the next few weeks of sailing, Magnus and the other Vikingars unceremoniously dumped the thralls in the ocean alongside the ships. When the first hit the water, it was obvious he couldn't swim, as he went straight down. To save his investment, the Viking whose thrall it was, had to jump in and rescue him. After that, the Vikings threw the end of a rope overboard, and told the thralls to grab onto it when they hit the water. By now, the long ship had its sail up, and the Vikings towed the line of unclean thralls behind the ship for quite a way.

Deeming the water-logged thralls to now be as clean as they'd ever been, the rope was pulled in and the thralls hauled on board. The sodden slaves were very fortunate that this was the summertime, so they didn't have to worry about hypothermia.

After bathing in the stream, Magnus put on clean clothes, combed his hair, used a toothpick and finally an ear spoon to clean his ears. After deciding that he was now as kempt as he would be, he headed to the village thing.

As he was walking around the market stalls, Magnus noticed a merchant's daughter working at her father's stall selling food. Magnus admired the girl for a while. She was tall, being only a few inches shorter than Magnus's six feet. She had a very statuesque figure, that any man would appreciate. Her hair was blonde and her face pretty. And she was a hard worker, efficiently selling her father's foodstuffs to the villagers. Waiting until foot traffic slowed a bit, Magnus walked up and asked to buy some salted pork, cheese and a flagon of fermented honey, called mead. While she was waiting on him, Magnus asked her name. She looked at Magnus intently for a moment before responding, "Esja."

"Esja, I am Magnus and I have a farmstead outside the village."

"You are the Jomsviking who decided to become a farmer."

Magnus laughed. "Yes, but I intend to still go a Viking sometimes!"

"I hope you have a strong wife to manage your farm when you are on your Vikings."

Gazing into her eyes, Magnus said, "I have not found one yet, but I'm looking."

Esja blushed at that. "I believe that woman would be proud to be your wife."

"I would like to meet and speak with your father."

Esja now blushed bright scarlet, which highlighted the deep blue of her eyes. "I think you should do so, as soon as possible."

Magnus located Esja's father Olfr and told him that he wanted to discuss the possibility of marrying his daughter.

Magnus had to convince the girl's kin that he would be able to provide them support and political influence once the marriage happened. Once it was agreed that an alliance between the two families would be satisfactory, the next step was to negotiate the bride-price. The bride-price consisted of three payments. The groom would pay the mundr and morning-gift, while the bride's family provided the dowry. The mundr was a payment to the father of the bride for the right of protection and legal guardianship which was held by her father until she was married. The mundr was calculated to be similar in worth to the girl's dowry.

Magnus knew the mundr was currently set at a minimum of twelve ounces of silver. However, that was only the minimum by law. Depending on the social strata of the bride's family, the wealth of the potential groom, and the desirability of the bride, it could be much more. As Olfr was a well-respected merchant, Magnus a relatively wealthy landowner, and Esja a very desirable young woman, the mundr would certainly end up being significantly more than twelve ounces of silver.

As Magnus and Olfr discussed the value of the mundr, they also discussed the second sum payable by the groom after the consummation of the wedding. This was known as the morning-gift.

The morning-gift was given to the woman as compensation for her sexual availability to her husband. The morning-gift was usually calculated in relation to the woman's dowry, being anywhere from one-third to one-half of the amount to the dowry. The morning-gift served to ensure the wife's financial support during the marriage, and thus she always had the use of the morning-gift. Olfr was well aware that his daughter was prime marriage potential. He and his brothers had already calculated the approximate values of her mundr and morning-gift. If he had been unimpressed by Magnus, Olfr would have given him numbers that were unrealistic for him to meet. Conversely, as everyone in the village knew about the wealth Magnus had earned as a Jomsviking, which made him very sought after as a potential husband, Olfr offered him realistic prices for both. After they both agreed to the mundr and morning gift values, they turned to discussing Esja's dowry.

The dowry represented a portion of her father's inheritance. The dowry would be administered by Magnus, but he would keep it as a trust which he could not squander. He also could not use it to replay any debts he might have. The dowry was intended in part for Esja's maintenance during the marriage but was reserved primarily as a sort of annuity which would be used to support her and her children if she became a widow.

With Magnus being a Vikingar, widowhood was always a strong possibility for his wife. Furthermore, if Magnus and Esja's marriage was not a happy one, the dowry would be returned to her in the event of a divorce. After the financial negotiations over the upcoming nuptials had been agreed to by Olfr and Magnus over several flagons of mead, Olfr excused himself to tell his daughter that she was to be wed. In Viking society, the daughter's agreement to the marriage was not required. However, in the instances the daughter didn't approve, the marriage was usually doomed. As Esja and Magnus had enjoyed their flirtations with each other prior to Magnus speaking to Olfr, Esja was quite pleased when her father gave her the news. She remembered her older sister telling her about the month-long period newlywed Vikings were left alone to drink mead wine made from fermented honey, called the honeymoon. Thinking about Magnus's impressive physique and rugged good looks, Esja imagined their honeymoon would be enjoyable, indeed.

After telling Esja the news, Olfr left to gather several friends. Now that the financial negotiations were complete, the arrangement was sealed with the handsal. Olfr's friends would be the witnesses to the agreements for the marriage terms. The oral agreement reached would have validity so long as at least one of the witnesses was alive. So, Olfr gathered his six closest friends in the village for the handsal. There was a set formula that was spoken by Magnus during the handsal, which sealed the contract. Once the handsal was complete, Magnus and Esja were now Viking newlyweds. Afterwards the bride's family threw an impressive wedding feast, complete with a roast boar and plenty of ale and mead.

Magnus and Esja retired to their farmstead and commenced their Viking honeymoon. During their respites from what honeymooners have always done, Esja made it clear that she would be undertaking numerous improvements to Magnus's bachelor pad. To Magnus, a house was nothing more than a place to sleep out of the cold. Esja turned to with a vengeance on showing him the errors of his ways. Magnus became well-aware that the majority of what he spent on Esja's bride-price, was to be spent on home improvements. Magnus was wise enough not to get too involved in what Esja was doing, and kept his opinions to himself, unless he was specifically asked. Esja also employed Magnus's thralls in the redecorating projects and home upgrades she embarked upon. As all Magnus had really used the thralls for around the house was cutting down, stacking and caulking the trees to build with, and the various daily functions of farm work, this was a new experience for them all. Since much of the labor was inside, the thralls seemed quite pleased with the change of pace. Esja had grown up with thralls in her household, so she was used to having them around. She was fair but firm. She would give them realistic chores to accomplish, would trust them to finish satisfactorily, but would also verify that they did so. Before Esja came to the farmstead, Magnus hadn't been particularly expressive with his thralls. He told them what to do and they did it. Magnus practiced communication by exception. Conversely, Esja's feelings were on full display, and the thralls all quickly learned to adjust.

By the time their honeymoon was over, the farmhouse had been transformed. Magnus had to admit that it was a substantial improvement. With most of Esja's household improvements being complete, she and Magnus had the thralls get back to the work that Magnus had them doing, farming and timber harvesting. Esja oversaw the female thralls working with the animals. She refined their techniques for making cheese from the cow and goat milk, which she was then able to sell in the village. Magnus spent his days overseeing the male thralls cutting timber that he then sold.

Magnus enjoyed the honeymoon immensely, as well as the domestic period afterward. However, after a few weeks of being a Norse farmer, Magnus began to hear the call of the North Sea. He had made no pretensions to Esja that he would renounce going on Vikings and felt now it was the time to tell her that when the season turned, a Viking he would go.

Chapter Three

When Magnus set up a Viking, he offered employment to most of the young men in the nearby villages. They all realized that this was their opportunity to capture thralls, pillage and loot whatever village they raided, and return with great wealth. Magnus had purchased his own longship, which was called a drakkar and would hold approximately 70 Vikingars. For a local raid along the area of the Vik, that was all he would need. However, for a Viking to the Isles of the Saxons and Gaels, he would need more warriors. Magnus would meet with other prominent Viking shipowners to recruit them for a raid. After he got their agreement, they would all then recruit enough Vikingars to man each ship. A Vikingar force of three long-ships would consist of approximately two-hundred men from the local area, thereby de-populating it of men for several weeks or months at a stretch.

This was the cost of doing the business of a Vikingar, but it could lead to problems. The Vikings were not a monolithic entity that would only raid outside entities. Each independent Viking kingdom consisted of several villages that would raid into other Viking kingdoms. When a large Viking raiding party left from a kingdom, it took most of the young men with it, which meant it was relatively defenseless against raids itself. Other Viking kingdoms would gain intelligence of this and plan their raids accordingly. As the only men remaining were the young, old and sickly, it fell upon the women to defend their villages. If they did not, they would watch their homes get looted, themselves raped, and they and their children enthralled as slaves. So, in addition to managing the farmstead while Magnus was away Viking, Esja would also serve as a shieldmaiden. Shieldmaidens were the female Vikings that would defend their homes and villages against raids. As a former Jomsviking, Magnus's military experience was tapped into to help train the village shieldmaidens in military arts. As Esja was a tall and strong woman, Magnus appointed her as the head shieldmaidens. While some probably assumed that this was favoritism due to her being Magnus's wife, once they saw Esja sparring with a wooden sword against the other shieldmaidens, they understood why.

Magnus believed that Esja was as good at fighting as some male Vikings and told her that if he didn't need her to manage the farm, he'd take her with him on a Viking. Hearing this, Esja blushed and asked him, "Are you sure that fighting is the only reason you'd bring me with you?"

"True, if you went with me, I doubt I'd get much raiding done, and the other Vikingars would be jealous."

Looking coyly at Magnus, Esja inquired, "You wouldn't share me with your comrades?"

He grabbed her around the waist. "I can assure you that I'd share you with no man." At that point, Magnus ended the day's shieldmaiden training and he and Esja then commenced to do what the recently married do.

For more than two weeks, the shieldmaiden training began each afternoon, after the village women concluded their morning chores at their farms and homesteads.

Understanding the physiological differences between men and women, Magnus modified the combat techniques he had learned as a Jomsviking. He understood that most women wouldn't have the upper body strength to wield a two-handed Dane or Sparth axe effectively. And to use a two-handed axe also meant that the shieldmaiden would have to let go of her shield, therefore, he disregarded that portion of instruction. Instead, he focused on the weapon with the most stand-off range. The spear. In all reality, the weapon with the most range was a bow and arrow. However, to master the bow and arrow took much longer than a fortnight, so he also omitted that. Instead, Magnus instructed the maidens on how to fight with a shield and a spear.

The first thing he taught was that combat was not a Holmgang, which was the one-on-one duel Vikings fought to settle disputes. Magnus made it clear that if the village was attacked, the shieldmaidens were to form a modified version of a Svinfylking, or a 'Boar Snout'. The Svinfylking was a version of the wedge formation used by the Vikings. The traditional formation consisted of heavily armed warriors and less-armored archers grouped in a triangle formation with the warriors in the front lines protecting the archers in center or rear. Since Magnus was foregoing the use of archers, he replaced them with reserve shieldmaidens that could take the place of frontline shieldmaidens that were wounded or tired.

Magnus had the women stand shoulder to shoulder, with each woman's shield protecting the women to her left. He emphasized that if a woman went down, her place had to be taken instantly by another shieldmaiden. In each woman's right hand, she held her spear. Magnus told them that they must use the roughly six-foot length of their spears to their advantage. They were never to throw the spear, as that would eliminate the spear's further use. Conversely, the attackers could then pick up the thrown spear, and use it against the shieldmaidens. Magnus explained that the attackers would try to come in close and use the curved bottoms of their axe heads to hook the shields and pull them down, thus exposing the maidens to attack. He reiterated numerous times that mustn't be allowed to happen. He demonstrated that a Viking coming in for an overhead swing with his Dane axe, would leave his midsection exposed. When that happened, the shieldmaidens would thrust their spears into the attacker's belly. As most Vikingars couldn't afford full armor, their stomachs would often be unarmored.

Wanting the shieldmaidens to fully understand the grim reality of what they may have to do, Magnus went into morbid detail. He explained that a spear thrust to the gut had multiple benefits. For one, unless the attacker was a Berserker, hopped up on mead and Scandinavian psychedelic mushrooms, the wound would instantly debilitate him. Secondly, wounds to the gut were extremely painful, making even the strongest scream in agony. Upon hearing such screams, the other attackers' morale would be shaken, making them more hesitant to press the attack.

Magnus went on to explain that there were several reasons men fought. First was honor and pride, and that neither could be gained in attacking women. Therefore, the Vikingars attacking the village were not doing it for honor or pride. A second reason might be for vengeance, which also satisfies honor. Magnus asked the shieldmaidens why they had attacked fellow Viking kingdoms? They all looked at him as if he were daft, and then Magnus said, "So, they aren't attacking you for vengeance." The third reason that men might attack them was for wealth. He said that was what he fought for as a Jomsviking primarily, with the other two often factoring in. He went on to explain that whereas wealth is a good inducement to go on a raid, once fellow raiders start falling dead, it is harder to keep fighting for that alone.

"If a raiding party encounters a strong foe while in the pursuit of wealth, then by defeating that foe, honor and pride would certainly be important. However, there would be no honor whatsoever to be gained by defeating a bunch of shieldmaidens, so pillage would be the attackers only motivation. If you show determined resistance and inflict enough damage on the attackers, they will soon decide to attack another village."

As part of the training, Magnus would have fellow Vikingars from the village stage feigned attacks. He provided the shieldmaidens the hafts of spears without the blades and told them to stab as hard as they would in a battle. He had the faux attackers wield wooden swords and axes and wear padded jackets to reduce the chance of injury. He watched as the skirmish occurred and critiqued the shieldmaidens performance afterward. They steadily improved, and after two weeks of dedicated training, were able to maintain their shield-wall while delivering accurate spear thrusts on the assailants, and quickly replace incapacitated women's places in the shield wall.

At the conclusion of the fortnight's training, Magnus told them that Esja would be their chief, and he appointed two other adroit maidens as her assistants. He also explained that the knowledge they had gained was perishable, and so two days each month they would have refresher training to maintain their skills. Magnus said that when he was on a Viking, Esja would run the training in his absence. "Never forget," he told them, "that if the village is attacked while we are away, you are the only thing preventing your homes from being looted, your elderly parents from being slaughtered, your children from being enslaved, and yourselves from being brutally gang-raped. All you know and love is at risk."

After the shieldmaiden's initial training was complete, and the long Norse winter began to wane, it was Viking time. During the winter, Magnus had already coordinated with fellow long-ship captains about the upcoming raid season. Magnus would strap on his cross-country skis to go visit the other Vikingars. The Norse had been using skis for many thousands of years, and even had Ullr and Skade, the God and Goddess of Skiing.

Magnus had been skiing since he could walk and was quite adept at it. He tried to select routes with substantial down-hill portions, for fun. Going downhill, Magnus was able to attain speeds of a horse at full gallop, which he found invigorating. Necessity breeds creation, and if it hadn't been for skis, Norsemen wouldn't be able to leave their homes in the winter months without sinking into fresh snow.

What Magnus was interested in was a Viking towards Leif Erickson's Vinland. Many years before, Leif who was the son of Erik the Red, had journeyed from the Viking settlement of Greenland to a new land he had named Vinland. Leif had come to Norway to tell about the new land, which he described as very temperate and well worth colonizing. Many Vikingars were now interested in journeying there, not only to colonize it but for the sheer adventure of exploring a new land. This was Magnus's primary incentive, to journey to a relatively unknown land, explore it and map it, and return as a legendary explorer. It sounded infinitely more interesting than farming.

Often, when Vikingars planned on going on a Viking, it was based on inducements of plunder and capturing thralls. Occasionally it was primarily for satisfying a Viking's inherent sense of adventure. In addition to fighting, Vikings were renowned as explorers. The sagas written about Vikings, which recorded their history for posterity, were usually about glorious deeds on the battlefield, and exploring new and distant lands. By now, the Vikings had explored almost the entirety of Europe, including the Mediterranean.

When he was a Jomsviking, Magnus had been employed by the Viking colony of Sicily and had fought in southern Italy. He had a served with Jomsvikings of the Rus tribe, who had colonized Russia. Anywhere a Viking longship could go, which was almost any ocean, sea, or river, they went. After Norseman Erik the Red had established colonies in Greenland, his son Leif Erikson had then explored further to the southwest and had established the colony of Vinland.

In Old Norse the word vin could mean "meadow or a pasture", which implied a pleasing and temperate land, providing for ample agriculture and livestock. Vinland could also mean a land where grapes grew, which meant wine could be fermented there. As it had been many years since these events occurred, every Vikingar understood that there was probably more unexplored land out there. Magnus had heard the Norse Skalds, or poets, read the sagas of Erik and his son Leif. These gave Magnus a burning desire to also go to and beyond, the places in the sagas.

After several meetings in the various longhouses of other prominent Vikingars over the winter, an expedition to go beyond Vinland had been planned. Magnus would be the leader and would supply one longship and crew. Two more wealthy Vikingars would also provide a ship and crew but wouldn't go on the Viking themselves. Instead, their firstborn sons would each captain their father's ships and would be Magnus's second and third in command.

The plan was to sail from the fjords of the Norse-land as soon as good sailing weather began, sailing first to Iceland to replenish, then on to Greenland to do the same. Each longship had at least one Vikingar onboard who had previously sailed to Greenland and could act as navigators along the coast. Magnus even had a Vikingar in his crew who had once been to Vinland. That would be the last known port of call where they would replenish once again before departing into the great beyond.

There were a few sagas about men who'd claimed to have sailed beyond Vinland, but they lacked credibility. Many thought that they were nothing more than some skald's overactive imagination. With three ships full of almost 200 Viking witnesses, Magnus knew that if he succeeded, no one would doubt the veracity of the sagas told about him.

After the expedition had been arranged, Magnus spent significant time with the other ship captains, ensuring they were prepared for their tasks. It was good that he did so. While they were both brave, well respected Vikingar warriors that had accompanied their fathers on ocean going raids, their mastery of seamanship skills were less impressive. They could both adequately sail and pilot a ship in fair weather, but that was about the extent of their ability. And it was almost assured, that the weather in the north Atlantic would be anything but fair.

From his many years of Viking experience, Magnus knew that it was cloudy approximately fifty percent of the days in the North Atlantic. Almost all Vikingars with substantial seagoing experience could navigate using the sun and the rudimentary sundials onboard all ships. If you knew roughly what time of day it was, and you could see the sun, you could tell what direction you were sailing. Since the northern Atlantic Ocean where Vikings sailed has nearly twenty-four hours of daylight in the summer sailing season, Vikingars did not have to rely heavily on the stars but did take full advantage of the sun to navigate. The sun rose in the east, and then marched its way westward as the day waned. The knowledge of how to navigate in those conditions could be learned in no longer than a fortnight. The difficulty arose when the sun couldn't be seen through the clouds or fog. This is where sunstones became lifesavers, which Vikings had used for several hundred years. By rotating the sunstone this way and that, the sky would appear to periodically brighten and fade. By looking for the patch of sky that was brightest regardless of the clouds, Vikings could identify where the sun was and then used the sundial to figure out which direction was north.

The Vikings had also learned that at noon every day, when the sun is highest in the sky, a dial in the center of the wooden shadow-boards, or compass they used, would cast a shadow between two lines on the plate of the compass. The seafarers would then measure the length of that noon shadow using scaling lines on the dial, and then determined their current latitude. Latitude is the angular distance of a place north or south of the earth's equator. Knowing the latitude, allows a sailor to specify his north–south position on the Earth's surface. Knowing their latitude would enable Magnus's navigators to stay on course during their long Transatlantic journey from Norway, to Iceland, to Greenland, and finally to Vinland. To learn all this took many cloudy days, which in Scandinavian winters, were not hard to come by.

The Viking mastery of the sunstone did not mean that they could only sail during the long summer days. They had also learned to locate the sun after sunset on a cloudy evening. Vikings would take a pair of sunstones, and when the two crystals are held up to the sky, the orientation of these patterns cast within the stones helped pinpoint the position of the sun below the horizon. Teaching mastery of this to the other boat captains was a complex process and took many, many days over the Norse winter. Between conducting these tutorials in the morning, and the shieldmaiden training in the afternoons, Magnus was ready to sail beyond Vinland, if for no other reason, just so he could take a break.

Chapter Four

The initial Shieldmaiden training was complete and the overcast navigation training had progressed very well. It had gotten to the point that Magnus felt that if the other two ships lost sight of his in a storm, then their captains could effectively navigate their way to the next port of call. The long winter was just about over, and it would soon be time for the final preparations.

It was the warming temperatures that lead to the event that would delay Magnus's departure by a few days. One morning a thrall of Magnus's was leading the cattle and sheep from the field to paw through the thinning snow for dead grass to eat. As they're were going by Magnus's neighbors' farmstead, a raven flew up in front of the cattle, which startled them and caused them to stampede towards the neighbor's farm. The neighbor's cattle were at the edge of a frozen stream taking a drink. Seeing Magnus's panicked cattle stampeding towards them, panicked them as well. The neighbor's cattle started their own stampede, directly onto the frozen stream. If this had happened at the height of winter, the ice would have probably held. As winter was almost over and the temperature were rising, it didn't. Once the panicked cows reached midstream, the ice gave way, and in went the cattle. Magnus's thrall was able to head his cattle off from following the other herd, but he could do nothing to save the neighbor's cattle. The cattle now had a reason to panic, as they couldn't swim through the ice to the streambank. The cows were mooing and bellowing with all their might, which drew Magnus's neighbor out from his longhouse. Thinking that the cattle were being attacked by wolves, the neighbor brought out his Dane axe. Seeing what was going on, the neighbor then used his axe to frantically chop ice by the riverbank to allow his cattle to exit the water. By doing so, he was able to save some of the strongest of his cattle, but several, particularly calves, were drowned. The neighbor was obviously upset at the loss of several valuable cattle. Seeing Magnus's thrall, he asked him what had happened. The thrall explained about Magnus's cattle stampeding and panicking the others. Hearing this, the still very upset neighbor then lost his temper and blamed the thrall for not being able to control his livestock.

Working himself into a bloodlust frenzy, the neighbor then picked up his Dane axe and buried it in the thrall's head, killing him immediately. While this was transpiring, Magnus's other thralls told him what was occurring. Magnus went to the river to see what could be done, and upon reaching it found his dead thrall with his neighbor standing over him. Magnus was told what had occurred and became very angry himself. His neighbor's name was Gunnar, and Magnus approached him." Gunnar, my cattle's stampede likely caused yours to stampede as well. I would have paid for your losses. However, you killed my thrall, who was not at fault. My thrall was much more valuable than your dead cows, so now you will have to pay the difference."

Hearing this, Gunnar spit on the ground and cursed. "I will pay you nothing you washed-up Jomsviking!"

Magnus looked at Gunnar coldly and said, 'Then I will see you at the Holmgang."

The hólmgang was a duel of honor, fought between two men, and it was associated with specific customs known as hólmgang-rules, which varied from place to place. All duels were conducted within a hólm, a bounded area which was often on an island. Each district had its own dueling-place, where traditionally such battles were fought. Within this area was secured a cloak approximately nine feet square, with loops in the corners. Pegs with heads were to be rammed in there. A series of three lines was cut into the ground around the outside of the cloak, each a foot apart. These three furrows, each a foot in breadth, were to be around the cloak, and at the edge of these borders were four posts which are called hazels. And when all this had been done the spot was called "hazelled." The entire marked out area in which the duel would take place was called the hólmhring. The total fighting area was no more than about twelve feet square. The hólmhring served both legally and ritually as a court of law. Traditionally, each contestant was to have three shields, and when they were destroyed then he must defend himself with his weapons only. He who had been challenged was to have the first blow. If either one stepped outside the hólmhring with one foot, then "he yields ground" was called. If a duelist stepped outside the hólmhring with both feet, then the judge would call it as "he flees." Each contestant was to have someone to hold his shield for him and would immediately pass him replacement shields, so he didn't have to step out of the ring.

There were several ways to be declared the winner of a formalized hólmgang. There were several line judges positioned around the hólmhring, to call out if one of the opponents' foot faulted. There was also a head judge that acted as umpire, who could call the fight over. He was always a well-respected Vikingar, usually a Jarl, whose authority both opponents agreed on. If one of the two was wounded so that blood flowed freely onto the cloak, then no further fighting was to be done. If one fighter yielded ground twice, the fight was called for his opponent. If a duelist was deemed as having fled at any time, his opponent was automatically the winner. The winner was also decided if one opponent was so exhausted, that he could no longer defend himself, or if both his sword blades broke. If the duel continued until each opponent had gone through all his shields, the judge would call it over. Although the ritualized hólmgang was not intended to be fatal, it involved men hacking at each other with swords, so death was not an unusual occurrence. In the event of there not being a clear winner, the opponents were told to strip to the waist, and he who was bleeding the most was declared the loser.

As the outcome of a hólmgang was considered law, the loser had to pay hólmransom. The hólmransom in the district Magnus lived was set at three marks of silver. The hólmransom was paid if both opponents survived. However, if either Magnus or Gunnar were killed in the duel, the deceased lost all his possessions, and the one who had killed him in the duel inherited them. So, if Magnus was killed, Gunnar would inherit the farmstead and everything on it, and vice-versa. Magnus didn't particularly desire to add to his farm by taking his dead opponent's land. Therefore, he had no desire to slay Gunnar during the hólmgang. However, Viking society was built on honor, and to dishonor someone would immediately result in a call for that individual's honor to be avenged. By killing Magnus's thrall and then refusing to pay for it, Gunnar had challenged Magnus's honor. Magnus refused to let that stand.

The usual weapon for use in hólmgang was the sword. Experienced hólmgang fighters carried two swords with them, one in hand and another on a thong looped about the wrist, which not only gave the duelist a "back-up" weapon if his blade became dulled or broken, but an extra length of iron with which to ward off blows when his shields were gone. When the hólmgang began, the challenged party struck the first blow. His opponent then struck one, and so on back and forth, until the combat was decided. As Magnus had challenged Gunnar, Gunnar struck first.

Viking shields were typically made of linden or basswood, relatively soft woods. Experienced hólmgang duelists knew the best strategy was to quickly destroy all three of their opponents' shields. As a Jomsviking, Magnus knew the value of a good shield and preferred his shields made of wood with greater resistance to splitting. Magnus's three shields were each made from European Black Poplar, Alder and Silver Fir wood. Magnus's second was a Vikingar who had accompanied him on many overseas Vikings named Alfr.

Prior to entering the hólmhring, Magnus and Alfr discussed strategy. They decided on the order the shields would be used, and they sharpened Magnus's sword with a whetstone. Magnus's swords were just as superior as his shields. Most Scandinavian swordsmiths made blades from many lumps of different types of iron with different properties, taken from different smelts. The smith selected the material that he needed, then shaped it, twisted it, and welded it to form a composite steel suitable for a sword blade. The process is called pattern welding. While this technique was effective in making swords, the metal was often relatively soft, and easily dulled, bent or broken. During his service as a Jomsviking, Magnus was introduced to the products of families of sword makers from Frankish lands along the lower Rhine River. Two of the most renowned sword-making families were the Ulfberht and Ingelrii. Their swords were prized by the Vikingars and were superior to other swords. Magnus believed that the Ulfberht family had invented a new way to forge blades that held a better edge and were stronger than others. These sword makers would inlay their name on a blade when making it, and these swords were highly prized. Magnus had acquired two of these swords as a Jomsviking, and he brought both to the hólmgang.

Gunnar, just as Magnus did, stood six feet and was likewise muscular. He delivered a mighty blow on Magnus' poplar shield that would have likely splintered softer wood. Magnus then went next with a blow that knocked a sizable chunk out of Gunnar's basswood shield. The two continued until Gunnar's first shield was splintered. He was handed his second shield and with his very next blow destroyed Magnus's first shield. The hólmgang continued until all of Gunnar's shields were destroyed and Magnus was on his last. The judge asked Gunnar if he wanted to quit and pay the ransom, and in an almost berserk like fury, Gunnar answered that he would rather die.

The fight continued with Gunnar blocking Magnus's blows with his second sword. The formalized aspect of the hólmgang now broke down as Magnus's final shield was smashed. As Alfr came into the ring to take the destroyed shield from Magnus, Gunnar broke from his appointed position on the opposite side of the ring. He leapt at Magnus swinging his sword. This was completely contrary to the ritualized formula of the hólmgang, where the fighters took turns swinging. It was supposed to be Magnus's turn, and by his actions the judge would declare Magnus the victor, if he survived. Alfr now showed his use as a second, by throwing Magnus's ruined Alder shield into Gunnar's face as he charged. This distracted Gunnar momentarily allowing Magnus to position his second sword to block the blow. The Jarl, who was the judge, was screaming that Gunnar had forfeited the hólmgang and for both fighters to retire to their corners.

With foam coming from his mouth, Gunnar yelled that he may have lost the hólmgang, but Magnus would lose his life! The hólmgang now devolved into the earlier Viking duel, called an Einvigi. This was an unregulated duel, fought with any weapons, in any location and by any methods. The combatants in an einvigi duel had no judge; rather, they relied on their strength and personal "luck" to decide the matter. The einvigi had been popular in earlier Viking periods, but had lost its place to the more formal hólmgang. Therefore, the einvigi had no standing anymore and Norse legal codes did not recognize it.

Duelists who participated in an extralegal einvigi could face legal ramifications. While Gunnar was surely aware of all this, he didn't care. He was playing for blood. With there being no more rules in play, Magnus and Gunnar would hack at each other until one or both, dropped. Gunnar drew first blood, when one of his blows ricocheted off Magnus's sword and gave him a glancing blow on his arm. Under the codes for a hólmgang, this would have ended the fight in Gunnar's favor. However, it had gone far beyond that by this time.

Realizing that this was now a fight to the death, Magnus reverted to being a Jomsviking. He feigned that his arm wound was worse than it was by dropping his second sword and crouching down. Seeing this, Gunnar then raised his sword over his head for a final downward swing. Magnus was waiting on this and stabbed his sword into Gunnar's chest. Viking swords were typically cutting weapons rather than thrusting, but Magnus's Ulfberht blade was so sharp, it could do both. It entered Gunnar's chest, piercing vital organs that dropped him.

Magnus pulled his sword out and looked at his fallen adversary. "Gunnar, you were surely a brave warrior, but not an intelligent one. If you'd been willing to pay me for the thrall you killed, then you and I could be drinking a cup of mead together. Instead, the Valkyries are taking you to Odin's Valhalla to sup there."

Looking at the Jarl who was staring in a stunned manner, Magnus said, "give my three marks of silver for the hólmransom to Gunnar's family to pay for his burial."

Magnus and Alfr then picked up their broken shields and left the hólmring.

Chapter Five

After spending the next few days absorbing Gunnar's farmstead and thralls into his own, Magnus and his Viking were finally ready to depart. They left the Vik and first sailed for a week to reach the Viking colony of Iceland. After procuring necessary supplies, they then sailed for Erik the Red's Greenland. After going over the ships one last time to verify seaworthiness, the Viking departed again. Another 800 vikas, or sea-miles, from the village at Eiriksfjord in Greenland, Magnus's expedition reached Vinland. The longships were fortunate to have favorable winds and they made the journey in three days, with none of the Vikingars having to row. Vinland was located Southwest of Greenland, and as the sagas had said, was relatively flat and temperate in the summer.

Vinland was not a large settlement and only consisted of eight buildings. The buildings, typical of Norse construction, consisted of sod placed over a wooden frame. The buildings were all either dwellings or workshops. The Village chief had the largest longhouse which measured ninety feet by fifty feet and consisted of several rooms. Three smaller buildings around its perimeter were workshops and living quarters for his thralls. The workshops included an iron smithy containing a forge and iron slag, a carpentry workshop, and a specialized boat repair area. One of the other workshops in the village housed of a spindle and a loom. Vinland was a permanent settlement containing families, not just a transitory waystation for Vikingar explorers.

When Magnus's expedition arrived, the villagers were excited to see them as it had been several weeks since another boat had stopped there. Magnus paid his respects to the village hetman at his longhouse. While his men were purchasing provisions from the villagers as well as contracting for ship and sail repairs, Magnus set down with the Hetman and some other high ranking Vinlanders to get information about what lay farther south. Instead of the standard mead, the Vinlanders drank wine made from various fermented fruits and berries that were native to this area. Magnus had to admit that it was a refreshing change from the fermented honey he usually drank.

As they drank, they also snacked on nuts Magnus had never tasted. The nuts came in a hard shell, that was cracked open with a rock to extract the tasty interior. Magnus was fascinated with these and inquired what they were and where they came from. The hetman took a sip of his wine and replied, "they are called butternuts and we get them from the Skraelings farther south."

Magnus had heard tell about the Skraelings when they had stopped in Greenland. They were the indigenous people that inhabited the new land where the Vikings settled. They didn't live in one place permanently, but moved about with the seasons, hunting and gathering as they went. During the warmer seasons when they were nearby, the Vikings would trade with them. The Vikings would get fresh meat and produce, which supplemented the foodstuffs they were able to produce in that climate. The Vikings had adapted their diet to the most available sources of protein in Greenland, which was the seal and various fish. So, the Vikings in Greenland and Vinland primarily subsisted on grains they grew, seal meat and fish, and milk and cheese made from the livestock they had brought with them from across the sea. Some of the smaller buildings in the settlements housed the livestock, along with the thralls. Magnus didn't think such sleeping arrangements were particularly pleasing to the thralls, but at least it kept them warm in the cold winters. While there were trees on Vinland which they used for boat repairs, they were not the butternut ones. The hetman said that those only grew much further south, where Magnus was planning on going.

Magnus asked if there was anyone at the village who had journeyed further south. He was told that there was one man called Håkon, who had been on a Viking in that direction. Magnus asked to speak with him and Håkon was brought over from the blacksmith where he worked.

While he was being retrieved, Magnus asked the hetman, "I would like to take Håkon with me as a pilot, if he's willing. Would you be inclined to do without him for a period of time?"

The hetman thought for a moment and replied, "Håkon is my best blacksmith, but I believe his apprentice might possibly be able to fill in."

Magnus took from his tunic a talent of silver and handed it to the hetman. Upon receiving it, the hetman smiled and said, "The only way to know if the apprentice can do it, is to let him try! So yes, if would be fine if Håkon wishes to go on your Viking."

Håkon arrived from the forge sweating and covered with black soot. They gave him some wine and Magnus spoke, "I understand that you've been a Viking further south."

Håkon sipped his wine and replied, "Aye, I went on one a couple summers ago. We sailed in a southwesterly direction in the bay south of us here, and then we rowed up a river that fed into the bay. It took us many days and we turned around as we were running low on provisions."

"Do you remember about how many days you journeyed?"

After thinking for a moment, said, "Indeed, we sailed in the bay for a bit over two days, passing around one island and then came to the mouth of the river that the captain had explored before. We then got out our oars to assist with moving up the river. By rowing, as well as using the wind when it was favorable, we navigated the river for a fortnight before we came to a very large lake, at least the size of the Vik back home. We sailed down the lake for a day until it entered another river, but then had to turn around and come back."

Magnus quickly did the math in his head and then inquired, "What drove the decision to return?"

Håkon rubbed his chin and replied, "Two main reasons. First, we were low on provisions. Our ship's quartermaster told the captain that we only had enough salted fish and seal meat to get us back to Vinland if we turned around now. To continue the Viking, we would have to stop at one of the Skraeling villages along the riverbank and barter for food. And our captain didn't wish to do that."

Magnus's ears perked up at this piece of information and he asked Håkon why the captain was reluctant.

"We were a relatively small Viking expedition consisting of only one karvi ship with a crew of thirty. And the captain had a nasty experience with the Skraelings before and didn't want to chance it again."

Realizing that this was possibly very important intelligence for his impending Viking, Magnus asked Håkon to elaborate.

"Our captain had been on a previous Viking as a crewman, whose purpose was to trade with the Skraelings to get such things as these." Håkon held up a butternut. "On that expedition, the Vikingars had pulled up at a Skraeling village to barter items they had that the Skraelings might want, particularly any colored cloth or metal object."

As Magnus made a mental note of commodities sought after by the Skraelings, Håkon continued, "The Vikingars had brought wine with them, which they shared with the Skraelings as they bartered. By the end of the night, several skins of wine had been consumed, and a few Vikingars had caught the eyes of some Skraeling maidens."

Magnus winced upon hearing this as he knew what probably happened next.

"Those Vikingars and the maidens retired somewhere more private, only it didn't turn out to be private enough. Whilst they were doing what men and women do, some of the male Skraelings heard it, and were none too happy. I don't know if these were the girls' husbands, fathers, brothers, or just jealous suitors. Whatever the relationship, they weren't happy. They roused up the rest of the Skraelings and they mounted an attack. This was not a Viking war party; they were there for trading. All the

Vikingars' shields were back on the ship at the riverbank, and the only weapons they had on them were short swords or daggers. The Skraelings don't, at least none that I know of, work with iron. They instead fashion blades made from quartz rocks, which they affix to clubs, arrows, war axes called tomahawks, and spears. These may sound primitive compared to our iron blades, but the quartz holds a very sharp edge, and they are very proficient at using it at a distance. Not only are they very skillful with their bows and arrows, but their atlatls need to be seen to be believed."

"I've never heard of an atlatl. What is it?"

"The atlatl is a spear-thrower that the Skraelings use. It consists of a wooden shaft with a cup at the end that supports and propels the butt of their spears. The spear-thrower is held in one hand, gripped near the end farthest from the cup. The spear is thrown by the action of the upper arm and wrist. The throwing arm together with the atlatl acts as a lever. The spear-thrower is essentially a fast-moving extension of the throwing arm, increasing the length of the lever. This extra length allows the thrower to impart force to the spear over a longer distance. Therefore, the spear ends up traveling at higher speeds over a farther distance. Using an atlatl, an experienced Skraeling can hurl a spear farther than a hundred steps, with good accuracy. A Vikingar's shield could possibly stop an atlatl spear from penetrating the skin, but his leather jacket would not."

Håkon went on telling what had happened, "So, the Skraelings grabbed their atlatls and bows and arrows, and commenced an attack on the Viking traders. As they were launching their spears and arrows from a distance, there was little the Vikings could do, other than make a break back to their ship on the riverside. By the time they'd reached it, and their shields, several Vikingars had been pierced by spears and arrows, including two that had been in the dalliance with the maidens. I have no idea if they were specifically aimed at by the Skraelings, or it was just their misfortune. Regardless, they were among a handful of others who didn't make it back to the longship. The ship's captain thought briefly about putting together a party to rescue those left ashore. But when he realized that several of those on the ship had also been wounded by arrows, none of those pierced by an atlatl spear had made it back to the boat, and that they were vastly outnumbered by the Skraeling warriors, he knew it was useless. So, the captain had them launch the boat back into the river, leaving their comrades to the mercy of the Skraelings.

"Of course, the process of pushing a longship into the water, leaves the crew temporarily unable to defend themselves. They were lucky in that once the Skraelings realized that two of the Vikingars left ashore were the ones who'd had their way with their women, that became their focus. The Viking captain was able to get its ship launched and into deep water. Fortunately, the Skraelings also didn't come after them in their canoes, from which they could have shot arrows and spears at the longship as long as they wanted. They left a half dozen Vikingars on the riverbank, and at least some were still alive."

Guessing the answer, Magnus asked anyway, "How'd they know they weren't already dead?"

"Because they could clearly hear the Skraelings finishing them off. The captain said that it sounded like the Skraelings were doing their equivalent of a blood eagle on the hapless Vikingars."

Magnus shuddered at hearing this. The blood eagle was a Viking torture technique only used on those deemed particularly vile, for example traitors, etc. To conduct a blood eagle, the victim is tied face down. The torturer then cuts off the victim's clothes, laying his back bare. The torturer next takes a sharp knife, and sticks it into the victim's back, next to his spine. The torturer is careful to not stick the knife in too deep, lest it pierce the heart or lungs. The torturer then proceeds to saw through the ribs, next to the spine. Each rib is cut through, then removed. After cutting all the ribs on one side, the torturer would then reach into the body cavity and pull the lung out. Next, the torturer would cut through all the ribs on the other side and pull that lung out as well. When the torturer was finished, the victim's exposed lungs made him look like he had bloody wings. When the torturer was finished, the victim was left to die, either of blood loss or shock. The whole procedure took several hours from the time it was started, until the victim was deceased, unless he died of a heart attack during it. Therefore, it was rarely implemented, and reserved for only the most severe punishment for a truly heinous crime. Few Vikingars had ever witnessed a blood eagle, but all had heard about it.

"The captain told us, that whatever method the Skraelings' used to kill the Vikingars, it took a long time, as the crew could hear them screaming in agony for quite a distance after they rowed away." Håkon took another sip of wine and cracked open another butternut then continued. "After his previous experience with the local Skraelings, our Captain's reluctance to barter with them for more provisions seems understandable."

"I agree with you on that," Magnus said.

"And that was just one reason we turned back. The other was Niagara." Seeing the uncomprehending look on Magnus's face, Håkon elaborated, "The name Niagara comes from a Skraeling word that means 'thundering water'. And it does. Have you visited the fjord with the Seven Sisters Waterfall back home?"

"I have, a truly awe-inspiring site."

"Then you'll have any idea of what Niagara is like. It is several hundred feet tall, and the river that flows down it is immense, being more than five acres across. With that volume of water flowing down it, you can understand why the Skraelings call it thundering water."

Magnus nodded his head emphatically and said, "Aye, I'm fairly certain that rowing up that might be a problem."

Håkon laughed. "Maybe if the boat had the God of the sea Njörd, and the goddess of the sea Rán, on board as passengers. Other than that, it would be a problem!"

They both laughed at that and Håkon continued. "If we were in a drakkar with a crew of sixty or more, we would have had the manpower to haul the boat out and portage it along the riverbank past the falls. Since we were in a karvi with only 12 pairs of oars, our entire crew only consisted of thirty men. So, even if we had plenty of food and the captain wished to continue the Viking, we lacked the men to do so."

Refilling Håkon's flagon of wine Magnus said, "This information you've given me will prove invaluable for my Viking. However, I still need a pilot to show me the way to the river. I talked to the hetman and he will allow it. Will you join my Viking?"

Håkon drained his flagon in one swig. "As I'm growing tired of hammering iron on an anvil, a Viking I will go!"

After securing Håkon's embarkation as the journey's pilot, Magnus and the other captains spent the next several days conducting ship repairs and bartering for provisions. After any tears in the sails had been sewn, the hulls caulked, and all the salted meat they could procure was loaded aboard the vessels, Magnus's Viking beyond Vinland was ready for launch. Usually on a Viking, either mead and or wine would be brought along to drink. This was not only because of the Vikingar's fondness for strong drink, but also because on a long oceangoing Viking, fresh water was hard to come by. And alcoholic drinks lasted longer than casks of fresh water, that tended to go bad after a while.

Since this Viking would only be in saltwater a short time before it entered a river, fresh water would be plentiful. Magnus also knew that at some point, they would need to barter with the Skraelings. Based on Håkon's recounting of what had occurred previously, Magnus thought that the lack of strong drink would be a benefit. The casks of mead that they had brought with them from the Land of the Norse, also made excellent bartering chips to procure salted meat from the Vinlanders. After the preparations were complete, the departure was set for the following morn.

Chapter Six

The day dawned bright and clear, but Magnus still had the other two ship captains determine their latitude using a shadow-board for practice. The wind was coming on their beam, and their long-ship sails billowed full, propelling them toward the great unknown. The bay they were in was full of fish, which the men trolled for by dangling baited hooks over the sides. Whales and dolphins were seen breaching frequently.

Keeping in mind his goal of becoming famous for this Viking, Magnus brought a Skald literate in Old Norse along as a recorder. The Skald's name was Dómaldr, and Magnus ensured that every day he wrote down something about their adventure and read it back. Up to this point, there hadn't been much noteworthy that had occurred, but Magnus felt that would change soon. After a day of sailing, they came to the island Håkon had told them about. Håkon had them steer to the north of it and then continued in a westerly direction.

After sailing through the night, they came to the end of the bay and Håkon directed them where to sail to find the mouth of the river. They entered the river and initially the wind was favorable, so they didn't need to row.

They navigated this river for more than a dozen days, stopping at night along the riverbank. Not knowing if the Skraeling were friendly or not, each night the stopped, Magnus had each boat post a pair of sentries by each ship's sleeping crew, to warn them in case of attack. They were not bothered, and by rowing and sailing for several days, they reached the big lake that Håkon had spoken of. They still had a favorable wind, so they kept the shoreline of the lake in sight to navigate by. After a day and night sailing, they reached the western edge of the lake, and Håkon stated that that the river with Niagara Falls fed into it nearby. Their journey from Vinland had taken approximately two weeks, and Magnus knew that soon, they would have to drag the longships out of the water and carry them by hand around the waterfall. Håkon had told him that there was a Skraeling village at the confluence of the river and lake. He also said that this wasn't the one where the previous Viking had run into trouble. Hearing that, Magnus decided to enter the village and ascertain if there were some way they could barter for fresh food.

The longships beached themselves next to the village and Magnus and Håkon, along with some Vikingars as security, got out. As they prepared to leave the lakeside, Magnus was surprised to see a Skraeling jogging towards them calling to them in Old Norse. As the man drew nearer, Magnus saw that while he was wearing the buckskin that most Skraelings wore, his features were definitely European.

Once he reached the party, he greeted them in Old Norse by saying, "Heill Vikingars, how goes your journey?" Magnus responded with the Old Norse greeting for good morning, "Gothan Morgun." Magnus appraised the man and noted that he was approximately 5'8" tall, had red hair and beard, that was turning to gray, and was probably in his late 40s. After sizing him up, Magnus said, 'You are the most Norse looking Skraeling I've ever met." The man laughed and replied, "Yes, I am Olav of the Icelandic Skraelings."

After sharing a laugh Magnus inquired, "Olav, how'd you come to be here from Iceland?"

"I was a crewman on a Viking several years ago that sailed here from Iceland. By the time we got here, the sailing season was late and so we overwintered here at this village. We were a relatively small group of around forty Vikingars and the village was very welcoming. They taught us the native language, and we all shared our ways for farming. We planted some seeds of barley and rye that we had brought with us, and the Skraelings introduced us to their primary crops, the 'three sisters,' by which they mean winter squash, corn, and climbing beans. Now in this village, the three sisters and Viking grains are harvested together."

"We also told them about how we fish. The Skraelings lack most metal, so they were amazed when we showed them how we used our fishhooks. They catch their fish in net-like obstructions called weirs, which they place across streams or rivers. The weirs are made of reeds, woven or tied together, and anchored to the bottom by poles stuck into the sand. With their tops extending above the surface of the water the weirs look very much like fences and are arranged in varied patterns designed to catch the fish. That winter, I was taken in by a native family and allowed to reside in their dwelling. By the time the winter was over, which wasn't quite so long as it is in Iceland, we had developed a very good relationship with this Skraeling village, who refer to themselves as the Wenro people.

When the winter ended all the other Vikingars returned to Iceland, except for me and two others who remained here."

"Why did you and the others stay here with the Wenro?"

"It was an easy choice for me, I married the daughter of the family I lived with that winter! I asked her if she wished to visit Iceland, and while she considered it, she decided not to leave her family. One of my mates was in a similar situation with a Wenro girl, and the other just said he had no desire to return to his father's hardscrabble farm in Iceland."

"How have you enjoyed the last few years with the Wenro?"

Olav scratched his beard and thought for several moments before answering, "I love my wife and she has already bore me two healthy children, a boy and a girl. There are several things I do miss, particularly mead and ale."

Magnus laughed and asked, "Have you had to switch to drinking wine only?"

Olav shook his head. "The Skraelings don't drink any fermented beverages."

Magnus was struck by this and asked, "If they don't drink alcohol, do they do anything when they socialize?"

"They smoke."

Not thinking that he had heard Olav correctly, Magnus asked him to repeat it." They smoke their tobacco," repeated Olav.

Magnus and the rest of his Vikingars looked at each other incredulously as Olav continued." Tobacco is a leafy plant that the Skraelings harvest, dry, crumble up in a hollow pipe bowl, light on fire and then draw the smoke into their mouths."

Hearing this, it was an incredulous Håkon who asked, "Why in the world would they bring burning fumes into their mouths?!"

"It doesn't seem intelligent does it? As you are visiting this village, it is likely that the Wenro will have a ceremony this evening where tobacco will be smoked, and you can observe."

Magnus asked Olav if the other two Vikingars were still in the village. "One of them also married a Wenro girl, and when a Viking came here last year, they left with it to go to Iceland. They haven't returned yet this summer, so they may have decided to remain there. My other comrade died defending the village from an Iroquois attack the winter before last."

Magnus asked, "Who are the Iroquois and why did they attack?"

"The Iroquois are a confederation of Skraeling tribes who are attempting to subdue nonaffiliated tribes, such as the Wenro. They are a large and powerful culture, and the Wenro are always concerned about another attack. Instead of just the summer, large scale fighting also happens here in the winter."

Magnus nodded and said, "It seems that the Wenro's relationships with their neighbors, are as fraught as any back home."

"Aye, truly." Olav then took Magnus and his party to meet the Wenro dignitaries and to admire the indigenous corn, squash and beans growing alongside the Vikingars imported barley and rye. As it had been several weeks since Magnus's Viking had departed Scandinavia at the beginning of the summer sailing season, the grain crops had been growing for months and were nearly ready for harvest. Olav made it a point to point out the large tobacco leaves growing alongside the grains. He said that it had been a good growing season for all the crops, and while the grains would be harvested soon, the Wenro would allow the tobacco to grow for another month or two before harvest and curing. When asked what curing meant, Olav explained, "As you can see, the tobacco leaves are currently big and green, you could hold a flame to them if you wanted to, and they wouldn't catch fire. After harvest, the leaves must be hung up out of the rain and allowed to dry, or cure, for a period of one to two months. At that point, the tobacco can be crumbled up and lit on fire in one of their hollow pipes. The smoke is drawn into the mouth, held there momentarily, then exhaled. In ceremonial situations, the pipe will then be passed on to the next man."

Listening to this Håkon said, "This seems a lot of trouble for something that is just going to be lit on fire!"

Magnus laughed. "There must be some benefit to going through this involved process."

"Aye, there is replied Olav, "there is a something in the tobacco that gives one energy and alertness. Even when they are on a war party and cannot smoke due to the noticeable aroma, the Skraelings will take the tobacco leaves and chew on them, to give them energy when fatigued."

Magnus looked at Olav and said, "While the thought of drawing smoke into my mouth doesn't seem appealing to me at all, you've been living with the Wenro for several years. If you recommend it, I'll try it."

Olav nodded his head and stated, "That is good, since you will be honored tonight at a ceremony with the Wenro chief, and a communal pipe will be passed to you. Put it to your lips, draw in a puff of smoke, hold it in your mouth then exhale. Word to the wise, don't draw the smoke into your lungs, if you do, you'll cough and look like an utter fool."

Magnus didn't think that intentionally inhaling smoke would be a concern, as he felt that would be the last thing he would do.

Olav continued, "Even though the Skraelings don't make mead, there are honeybees here. I occasionally find a hive, take the honeycomb, put it in a bucket with water, let it sit in the sun and turn to mead. I don't have much, and save it for ceremonial occasions, like tonight."

"If it is a small amount of mead, that'll be fine." He went on to explain that the reason he didn't bring any mead on this Viking, was because of what Håkon had told him. After listening to Håkon's retelling of the six drunk Vikingars that were slaughtered by the Skraelings, Olaf said, "I will bet you that it was those Iroquois bastards!"

To which Håkon only said, "It may be, it very well may be."

After being introduced to the Wenro higher-ups, and touring the village and crops, Magnus was taken to Olav's house to meet his family. Magnus met Olav's Wenro wife and was told that her name was 'Dove' in the native tongue. Magnus had to admit that she was a very attractive woman and could understand why Olav had stayed here to be near her. His two children, one about four and the other around two years old, were both healthy and good looking. Magnus observed that the combination of Norse and Skraeling blood made for fine looking children.

When the introductions were complete, Magnus asked Olav, "Did you leave a wife and children back home?"

Olav shook his head. "I once had a fine wife back home, but she died of cholera. We had two daughters, one of whom died of typhoid fever when she was three. The other, who was staying with my sister while I was on a Viking, was taken in a raid to be a thrall. I imagine she is probably some man's frille now, as she is an attractive young woman. All those are reasons that I really had no desire to return to the land of the Norse."

That evening Magnus and his officers were invited to the Wenro chief's longhouse for dinner. Magnus was introduced to the chief by Olav, who was acting as the translator. Olav said that the chief's name was Saundustee Onnonhou, which meant 'Water Man' in the Wenro language. Olav explained that the chief had been born a few weeks prematurely while his mother was aboard a canoe traveling to visit relatives across the lake, hence his name. Saundustee was tall, well built, with black hair that was in the most unusual style Magnus had ever seen. The hair was relatively long on top but was shaved along the sides. Magnus asked Olav if that haircut had any significance.

Olav said, "Yes, it's called a 'mohawk'. It is named after one of the Iroquois tribes but is worn by many Skraeling tribes in this area. The hair on the sides is plucked out, not shaved, by the warriors' wives when they are preparing to go on the warpath. They also pluck any facial hair the men get, which isn't much. They use tweezers made of bone to remove the hairs."

Magnus cringed upon hearing that. "Why do you pluck instead of shaving?"

"Because they don't work in iron, so the only blades they have are made of rock. I guess they could try shaving with a sharp obsidian rock, but that wouldn't be enjoyable."

Magnus shuddered as he agreed.

Olav continued, "The Wenro were amazed upon seeing my sword and Sparth axe when I got here. They couldn't believe how sharp the blades were and fascinated when I showed them how to sharpen the blades with a whetstone. I made a gift of my sword to Saundustee, as he was letting me stay in his longhouse and marry his daughter. I shortened the handle on my axe to make it more useful for cutting timber to build their lodges and clear land for cultivation. As I am living amongst them now, it seemed the least I could do."

The Wenro and Vikings had a delicious feast consisting of corn, pumpkin, and bread made from Olav's imported grains. The protein dishes consisted of numerous lake-caught fish including salmon, trout, northern pike, bass, walleye and carp. Finally, they dined on venison. The Vikingars were most impressed by the roasted ears of corn and strips of pumpkin, as they had never eaten either before. Olav also broke out his carefully hoarded mead, which was enough to provide one or two drinking gourdfuls' to all the diners.

As Olav had said, at the conclusion of the feast, Saundustee brought out a long clay pipe, ceremoniously filled the bowl with shredded tobacco, and was given a lit ember to ignite it. He took a few puffs on it, to ensure it was lit, and then passed it to the man to his right, who also took a few pulls on it. This procedure continued, until it had been passed to every man, Wenro as well as Vikingar, in attendance. Magnus was careful to do as Olav advised, and only hold the smoke in his mouth, before blowing it out. After the pipe bowl had been emptied and refilled, it was passed around again as they all sipped their mead. Magnus had to admit, that smoking the tobacco in the mixed company of Vikingar and Wenro warriors, was an enjoyable experience. He did feel a bit of a headrush after taking his pulls but didn't find it unpleasant in the least. A few of the Vikingars didn't heed Olav's warnings and breathed in the smoke. This invariably incurred a coughing and gagging fit, which amused the Wenro to no end.

After the pipe had been smoked and the mead drank, the ceremonial feast drew to a close. Magnus turned to Olav. "Tell Saundustee that we enjoyed this evening very much." Olav smiled knowingly and replied, "That is good, as this ceremony was also an invitation for you to join the Wenros' warpath against the Iroquois!"

Chapter Seven

Not being sure of what he'd heard Olav say, Magnus asked
him for clarification.

"The reason the warriors' Mohawks are freshly plucked;
is they are preparing to attack an Iroquois' village in
revenge for their attacks on Wenro villages. Since my
arrival here, I have regaled the Wenro with tales of Viking
battles and Saundustee has always said that if he had a
few dozen Vikingars, he'd deal with the encroaching
Iroquois. He believes that the arrival of a couple hundred
Vikingars is the Great Spirit's will. Of course, you could
say no to his invitation, but if you do, you should leave the
village immediately and take me with you, as I won't be
welcome here anymore either."

Magnus told Olav to give him a few minutes to speak
with his captains. Magnus drew close to the captains and
told them, "We have been asked to join our hosts in an
attack on a rival Skraeling tribe. I never envisaged this for
our journey, and I will not order you and your men to come
along. This will be voluntary only. Go back to your long-
ships, tell your crews of this, and inform me in the
morning of how many of your men wish to join me in a
Skraeling war." The ships' captains departed the
longhouse.

Magnus told Olav, "Tell Saundustee that I will
definitely join his attack, and in the morning, I will know
how many others will as well."

"I will let him know, and Saundustee has invited you to sleep here in his longhouse."

Magnus thanked him and returned to his ship to retrieve his bed roll. Back at the ship Magnus also spoke with his Skald so that he would record all the events that had taken place today. Magnus's Saga was shaping up to be a good one.

The next morning Magnus awoke and went back to the ships to talk with his captains. He felt fairly certain that at least a few Vikingars would be up for a fight, but how many remained to be seen. Over breakfast, Magnus found out that while roughly one-hundred men had no desire to participate in a fight that had nothing to do with them, the other one-hundred or so men were more than willing.

Both of his captains wished to accompany him on the warpath, but upon realizing that roughly half of his Viking would be remaining behind, Magnus had other ideas. Looking at the two captains, whose names were Baldr and Fólki, he said, "You're both brave Vikingars and I'm not surprised you wish to fight for our hosts, but I have an important mission for one of you. While one of you can accompany me to the fight, I need the other one to gather critical information. When we continue our Viking, we will sail up the river until we reach the Niagara waterfall, we've heard so much about."

"Once there, we will have to drag our boats ashore, and portage them up the river past the waterfall, where we can put them back in the water. We should have enough crewmen to manhandle the boats along the riverbank, but how difficult that'll be remains to be seen. I need one of you to journey up there to the waterfall, beach your boat, walk along the riverbank to learn how far we'll have to portage, and gather any other useful information." After giving them the mission, Magnus let them alone to discuss it.

After speaking together for a few moments Baldr and Fólki said, "We have discussed it and have an answer for you. Baldr will accompany you on the attack on the Iroquois, I will take the remainder of the men in my boat, and we will conduct reconnaissance."

"Very well, we will kill many of the Wenro's enemies while we also gain critical information for our continued journey. This bodes well for our Viking."

After breakfast, Magnus approached Saundustee's longhouse with Olav to translate. As this was an important discussion, Saundustee brought out his pipe and filled it. Once lit, he told Magnus and Olav to start.

Magnus, speaking through Olav, said, "I, along with one-hundred of my warriors will accompany you on your attack on the Iroquois." Once this was translated to him, Saundustee was ecstatic, as this more than doubled his number of available warriors. Magnus continued, "Tell Saundustee that as the Wenro and Vikings have different fighting styles, I will need time to observe, and determine how best to use my men. So, we cannot attack immediately,'

Olav explained all this to Saundustee who nodded his concurrence. Magnus also told Olav to inform Saundustee that as soon as practical, he wished to watch a rehearsal of how the Wenro warriors fought. Saundustee replied to Olav that Magnus could watch one today if he'd like. Magnus said that would be excellent. Saundustee finished by saying he would bring some of his warriors up to a recently harvested corn field, and the practice would go there. Magnus left to get his men, as did Saundustee. After gathering their respective groups, they met at the field.

Once they all gathered at the harvested field, the Wenro began their practice skirmish. Saundustee had several straw men emplaced at the far end of the field, to portray the Iroquois. The Wenro warriors didn't fight in a tight formation as did the Vikings, but in a more dispersed manner. They commenced their attack by launching arrows from their flatbows which had a range of over two hundred yards.

At nearly the same time as the archers were firing, other Wenro were launching spears with their atlatls. The atlatl spears were approximately four to five feet in length, and Magnus was impressed watching how much mechanical advantage the atlatls gave the spearmen. The spears flew for well over a hundred yards with significant accuracy. After the first arrows were shot and spears were thrown, several strawmen looked like porcupines. After launching their projectiles, the Wenro warriors dropped their bows and atlatls, took their tomahawks and warclubs that they carried with straps, and commenced individual attacks on the strawmen, all the while emitting blood curdling war-cries.

After observing the Wenro conduct a couple of these practice runs, Magnus told his men to form up to show their hosts how the Vikingars fought. Magnus had them form up in a Svinfylking, or a 'Boar Snout' formation. This was a triangular formation that the apex was composed of a single file. The number of warriors then increased by a constant in each rank back to its base. The swine array could be used as a wedge to break through enemy lines. Several Svinfylking formations were grouped in a side by side appearing something like a zig-zag to press or break the opposition's ranks. The swine array's effectiveness was based on monumental shock. Magnus had his approximately eighty men form a Svinfylking twelve rows deep, with each row in front having one less man, until it reached the lone Vikingar at the Apex. Each Vikingar held his shield in his left hand, which also protected the man to his left. After the Svinfylking was formed up, Magnus had them advance in formation at a slow jog down the field.

The Wenro, who had never fought in formation, were duly impressed by this technique. By way of instruction, Magnus had Olav ask the Wenro to form up in a line down the field to feel the impact of the Svinfylking. Magnus had the Vikingars sheath their swords and only hold their shields. Magnus asked the Wenro to stand their ground as long as possible and told the Vikingars to slow their pace to a brisk walk, but the outcome was inevitable. The Svinfylking moving at a fast walk slammed into the Wenro and knocked them asunder. Several Wenro who had locked arms were knocked down as one unit and the Vikingars did their best to not step on them, but that happened as well.

After demonstrating the Svinfylking to the Wenro, Magnus formulated a plan of action. Usually in a Viking Svinfylking, the less-armored archers were grouped in the middle or back of the triangle formation. That way, the warriors in the front lines protected the archers in center or rear. Since few of Magnus's Vikingars brought bows and arrows, the Wenro archers and spearmen would fill that role. Magnus would have them move along behind the Svinfylking, firing arrows and throwing spears over the Vikingars heads as they advanced toward the Iroquois warriors. Magnus explained his plan to Olav and had him tell it to Saundustee.

Saundustee was impressed and the only request he voiced was that once they reached the Iroquois warriors, the Wenro could come from behind the triangle and attack with their tomahawks and warclubs. Magnus answered that he hoped that they would do so.

Both Saundustee and Magnus went to brief their groups on the plan and ensure everyone understood it. One of Magnus's men expressed concern that once the Vikingars reached the Iroquois and a melee began, the Vikingars wouldn't be able to tell the difference in an Iroquois and a Wenro.

Magnus agreed that was a valid concern and brought it up to Saundustee. After pondering it, Saundustee said that if Magnus would give him colored cloth, he would have his men braid it into their Mohawks, so the Vikingars could easily identify them. Magnus agreed that was a capital idea and cut up some of the red cloth they had brought for trade and gave the strips to the Wenro.

Magnus and Saundustee asked their parties if anyone saw other problems that needed to be addressed. A few minor things were identified and then worked through. Magnus and Saundustee agreed that they would conduct several walk-throughs over the next day, with everyone that would be in the attack participating. Magnus said that his warriors who weren't going on the raid, would play the parts of the Iroquois in the mock battles. All participants carried tree branches in place of edged weapons. Even so, Magnus told his Vikingars not to strike with full force on the unarmored opponents, as a broken bone would take them out of any upcoming battles.

For the next several days, the Viking and Wenro warriors practiced their combined attacks on the faux Iroquois. Magnus, using Olav to translate, would frequently ask Saundustee for his input. After both Magnus and Saundustee were satisfied with the preparations, the date of the attack on the Iroquois village was selected. Saundustee told Magnus that they would attack a village of the Onondaga people, part of the Iroquois nation. It was an approximately a hundred miles journey to East, via the lake. Saundustee said that the Wenro would place one Viking in each of their canoes and spend several days rowing on the lake to reach the village.

Hearing this, Magnus came up with a proposal. He said to Olav, "Tell him that instead of one Vikingar sitting in the bottom of every Wenro canoe, all the Wenro warriors can embark on our two long-ships and we will sail to the attack."

Saundustee pondered this a moment and replied, "The Cayuga tribe resides next to the Onondaga. The Wenro are on good terms with the Cayuga. We can sail your boats to the Cayuga village on the lakeside, disembark, and then march the rest of the way for the attack." Magnus thought this idea was sound and agreed.

The day prior to the attack, Saundustee told Magnus that during the evening, the Wenro women would freshly pluck the warriors' mohawks. He inquired if Magnus wished to have the women pluck mohawks for the Vikingars as well? Magnus responded that he doubted if any of the Vikings wished to sit through the pain of having most of their hairs plucked out, but that several might cut their own mohawks with their knives, to show solidarity with the Wenro.

Immediately after that conversation, Magnus took out his knife, ran a whetstone over it, and proceeded to cut his own mohawk. He used a polished brass shield boss as a mirror to see what he was doing. As this was the first time Magnus had ever cut any of his hair down to the skin, he nicked himself several times in the process. After finishing cutting his mohawk and washing off the blood, Magnus showed it to his men.

His men had no idea that their leader was contemplating effecting the haircut of their native allies and their reaction was appropriate. The uproarious response evidenced by his men was exactly the prebattle morale boost Magnus had hoped for. The jocularity was contagious, and soon nearly every Viking and Wenro had come by to admire it. Several of the Vikingars were so inspired by his example, that they proceeded to give each other mohawks. The Wenro, who had never witnessed Europeans with blonde, red and brunette mohawks, were likewise jubilant. That evening, the Wenro and Vikings shared a pre-battle meal of fresh venison, corn and pumpkin. Olav shared some of his valuable mead with the officers of both parties, and afterwards, out came the ceremonial pipes. Magnus had smoked several times by this point and had to admit that he rather liked the mild rush pipe smoking gave him. The men then all turned into their bed rolls.

The next morning, as his men prepared the two assault ships to sail, Magnus spent some time with the Captain remaining behind. "Fólki, we will sail up the lake for about a day before we reach the Cayuga village. Once there, we will unload and then move by foot for another couple of days before we reach the Onondaga village we'll attack. After the attack is complete, we'll return to our boats, and thence here. The entire raid should take less than a week, start to finish. The Wenro are understandably concerned about leaving their village unprotected during this time, since all their warriors will be with us. Therefore, when you depart to conduct your reconnaissance of the Niagara, ensure that you leave at couple of dozen Vikingars here to defend the village." Fólki nodded his head in agreement and replied, "I was planning on leaving about three dozen behind, to reduce the amount of provisions we'll eat on the journey to Niagara."

"Even better." Feeling confident of the all the plans, Magnus had Olav tell Saundustee about the Vikings remaining behind for security and went to verify the ships' state of preparation. After the Wenro warriors said their goodbyes to their families, it was time to sail.

The Wenro had never been on an ocean-going vessel, and they were amazed by the scale of what they considered 'giant canoes'. They set sail at around noon and fortunately, the wind was blowing strongly on their beam or broad reaches, so they made good time sailing up the lake. They reached the Cayuga village just before nightfall. Saundustee had sent some of his respected elders to the village several days before to tell them of his upcoming visit. The Wenro were currently on good terms with the Cayuga, but Saundustee didn't trust them enough to tell them of his planned assault on the Onondaga. Instead, he instructed his elders to just tell them that Saundustee wanted to show off his new Vikingar friends to the Cayuga.

When they arrived at the Cayuga village, they were waiting. The Cayuga chief, who Olav told Magnus was named Onangwatgo, was there personally to greet them. He warmly greeted Saundustee and was then introduced to Magnus. The Cayuga, like all the other Skraeling tribes in the vicinity, were well aware of the Vikingars in their 'giant canoes' being in the area. Onangwatgo told Olav that while he had seen a few other Viking groups sail along the lake over the years, none that were so robust as this one. Saundustee then stated that this was only part of this group, as another ship was back at the Wenro village. Onangwatgo was duly impressed and was proud to show off the Cayuga village to the Wenro and Vikings. After he gave them a tour of the village and their bumper crops, which were growing as well as at the Wenro village, he invited them for to dinner.

This feast was like what they had eaten at the Wenro village, and also included butternut squash, in addition to the pumpkin. And just as at the Wenro feast, the tobacco pipes were brought out and passed around. By now, the Vikingars were well versed in the use of smoking tobacco, and none embarrassed themselves by coughing. During the pipe smoking, Olav heard Onangwatgo ask Saundustee about the warriors freshly plucked mohawks.

Realizing that he couldn't hide the fact that the Wenro were on the warpath any longer, Saundustee admitted that they were going to attack the Onondaga. Saundustee also told Onangwatgo that if he didn't wish the Cayuga to be implicated in the Wenro's assault, they would load the ships and attack from the lake. Onangwatgo said that the Cayuga had also been battling the Onondaga, and Saundustee was welcome to cross Cayuga lands to make the attack.

Håkon, who had also been sitting in earshot, later told Magnus that he remembered hearing the word Onondaga when he was told about the Skaelings previous killing of the Vikingars. Magnus thought this excellent information to share with the Vikingars, as if they thought that the Onondaga had tortured to death several of their fellows, it would make their participation in the fight, personal.

The last order of business that evening was Saundustee telling Magnus that the following morning, he would send a scouting party consisting of a handful of warriors to reconnoiter the approach to the Onondaga village. Magnus stated that he would like to include a pair of Vikingars, so they could relay their gathered intelligence to him personally upon their return. Saundustee agreed and Magnus went to Baldr and told him to pick two Vikingars to accompany the Wenro. Magnus admonished Baldr that the two would leave their shields and armor behind, as this was to be a fast-moving scouting party. Baldr said he understood and would select two of his fleetest men to go. The night's feast and business finished, everyone retired to sleep.

The next morning, the four Wenro and two Vikingars who were to conduct the reconnaissance departed along with a couple of Cayuga to show them into Onondaga territory. The remaining Vikings spent the day sharpening swords and axes and mentally preparing for the fight. The majority were veterans who had seen combat before, but there were a handful of young Vikingars who were on their first Viking. They were unsure what the morrow would bring and asked many questions of their more experienced fellows. Invariably, the veterans told them to rely on their training and to keep an eye on the experienced Vikingars. Having all once been new to the test of battle themselves, the veterans humored the neophytes and did their best to explain to them the sights and sounds they could expect. They reminded them to never break the shield wall until told, to always keep their shields up, as it not only protected them but the man to their left.

"Make sure an Iroquois warrior is dead before you step over his body. Many a Vikingar had been stabbed from underneath by a supposedly dead enemy."

"The screams and groans of the wounded will be the hardest thing for you to endure but endure it you must." The veterans said that the Iroquois Skraelings were renowned archers, and that was probably the first weapon they'd face. The Vikingars' shields, helmets, chainmail and lamellar armor would stop most arrows, but the veterans admitted that an occasional arrow would pierce the skin. If an arrow gets through your armor, leave it in there for the time being. Pulling it out only increases bleeding.

"The most important thing to remember is that you are Vikingars. Make sure you do all you can to fight like one."

Magnus spent the day amongst his men and overheard many of these exhortations. By the end of the day, the preparations were as complete as they would be, and all that remained was for the reconnaissance party to return and relate what they'd found.

They were supposed to return to the Cayuga village sometime that night, but by dawn the next day, they had not returned. A concerned Saundustee gave them till noon, but they still didn't arrive. At that point Saundustee and Magnus both agreed that something must have gone terribly wrong with the reconnaissance element, and they should commence their attack without delay. Led by the same two Cayuga that had escorted the scouting party into Onondaga territory, the combined war-party of nearly one hundred and sixty men set off. As agreed to previously, the more heavily armed Vikingars were in the middle of the formation, and the much lighter Wenro moved on the flanks, to prevent an ambush.

After crossing into Onondaga territory several miles earlier, it was one of the flanking parties that found them. The four Wenro and two Vikingar scouting party had been ambushed and were all dead. As this had been a close-range fight, all six had been killed by warclub or tomahawk blows.

Magnus had seen more dead men that he could count, but this was the first time he'd seen ones with their scalps removed. All six had the skin at the top of their foreheads cut, peeled off the skull, and then cut through at the back of the head. The result was that all four of the Wenro, who wore mohawks, had all their hair removed, and that the two Vikingars had their top hair gone, but the hair on the sides remained.

The Vikingars had never witnessed this before and asked Olav about its significance. "The Skraelings call it either hononksera or kannonrackwan, and it is the removal of the onnonra, or top of the hair. It is usually referred to as a scalping. After taking the scalp, they dig a hole in the ground and make a fire. Over the fire they dry the scalps until they look like parchment. After they are dried, they are stretched on hoops, painted, and decorated. They are considered trophies of war to be publicly displayed on canoes, cabins, and palisades."

While Magnus was incensed over the death of two of his men, he was also intrigued at the practice of scalping. He asked Olav, "Do all the Skraeling tribes' practice this? I'm sure I would have noticed scalps if I saw them at the Wenro village."

"As far as I know, they all do practice scalping, but how each tribe does it will differ. When Wenro warriors return successfully from the warpath, the tribe celebrates with dancing. Both men and women participate in the Scalp Dance. Each tribe's dance was somewhat different, but for the Wenro, scalps are brought into the village on long poles which were later decorated. The dancing is exuberant, but since it is a ceremony in a dance format, it follows a certain order and choreography. The Medicine men sing and beat drums while men and women dance in concentric circles around the scalps. Sometimes dancers will mock the scalps or mimic hunting down the person to whom the scalp had belonged."

"When dancers get tired, a woman who had lost a male relative in battle would narrate the particulars of the battle and how her loved one had died. After that, she might ask whose scalp she has. Or she might take the scalp from the pole and spread it across her shoulders and say, 'and now whose scalp is across my shoulders?' The sense of victory is an important component of the dance. These dances can continue at intervals for several days or weeks. Some Skraeling tribes will then decorate their village with the scalps. The Wenro however, eventually bury the scalps, which is the reason you haven't seen any. If our attack on the Iroquois is successful, you will witness many scalps being taken as well as the dances when we return to the village."

As the Iroquois had stripped the bodies of everything as well as taking the scalps. Magnus asked Olav, "What will the Wenro do with their corpses?" Olav replied, "For right now, they will place them up in trees to keep them away from animals. One the way back from the Iroquois village, they will take them home. After we return, the bodies will be buried for a period to let the flesh decompose. After a certain period, the skeletons will be disinterred and cleaned. Then a ceremony will take place in which the skeletons will be interred in a final mass burial that will include furs and ornaments for the dead spirits' use in the afterlife." Magnus realized that this was very similar to a well-to-do Vikingar's burial in a longship, also invariably with items for his use in Valhalla.

"As we won't be doing that with our two dead Vikingars, ask Saundustee if we have time to bury their bodies here, so that Odin's Ravens won't eat their flesh?"

After speaking with Saundustee, Olav said, "The Iroquois know we are coming and are preparing. The time required to bury our warriors will make no difference either way."

After the burial was complete, Magnus called up one of the Vikingars whose father was a Godi, or Norse priest and asked him to say some funerary rites. The brief ceremony complete, the Vikingars picked up their shields and joined the Wenro to continue their approach to the Iroquois village.

The combined force halted once it grew dark and made camp. All the warriors had brought dried meat to sustain them on their march, and numerous creeks provided water. As this was a war-party, both Magnus and Saundustee stationed security elements on all sides of their camp, to prevent a surprise attack that night.

They were not bothered and arose the next morning to continue their movement to the Iroquois village. They reached the outskirts of the village that afternoon after having walked approximately forty miles over two days. After intercepting the Wenro and Viking scouting party, the Iroquois had removed their own women and children from the village and sent them elsewhere. The village was a large one, and its nearly two hundred warriors were awaiting the assault.

The Onondaga didn't sit idly by awaiting the attack. They had sent out their own scouting parties to warn of the Wenro's approach. Their presence was announced by an Iroquois arrow piercing the chest of a Wenro in the flank security element. Both sides emitted ear piercing war cries and the Wenro security element launched themselves on a similarly sized Iroquois group.

The battle was not hard to find due to the incessant war whoops the warriors emitted. It only took the main party consisting of the other Wenro and all the Vikingars a few minutes to reach the scene of the skirmish, but it was already over.

The Iroquois element had retreated back to their village leaving four fallen Iroquois and a similar number of dead and wounded Wenro. As Olav had described to Magnus, the Wenro were in the process of scalping the vanquished Iroquois. Magnus watched how they did it and noted that one of the Iroquois wasn't even dead while he was scalped. The Wenro warrior doing the scalping kneeled in the center of his back, while two other Wenro held his arms. The Wenro on his back, made a couple of quick slices with his Obsidian knife, and then held aloft the unfortunate Iroquois' mohawk. The scalping Wenro let out a whoop after he had it, matched in its intensity by the now scalped but still alive Onondaga's shriek of pain.

After removing the Iroquois' scalps, the flanking element rejoined the main party for the final attack on the village. The surviving scalped Iroquois was left alive, writhing in pain from his wounds and scalping. Seeing that the Wenro were going to leave him like that, Magnus felt compelled to do something about it. He took out his sword, approached the pitiful Iroquois, and stabbed him in the chest. Magnus then rejoined the war-party and finalized their plan of attack.

Wenro scouts said that the main Iroquois village was just up the glen, and that the Onondaga warriors were formed up in a line awaiting them. Magnus had the Vikings assume their Svinfylking, and Saundustee had the Wenro form in the rear. The combined unit moved at a slow jog down into the village. The loose formation of Iroquois was stunned to see the Svinfylking consisting of shield bearing Vikingars approach them. As rehearsed, approximately two hundred yards from the Iroquois, the Svinfylking paused, allowing the Wenro with bows to shoot over and around them. The Svinfylking then proceeded slowly forward, allowing the Wenro with atlatls to throw their spears. At this point in time, the Iroquois had transitioned solely to the bow and arrow, which they fired at the approaching Svinfylking. As the veterans had told the recruits, most arrows impacted the Vikingars' shields or passed overhead into the ranks of the unprotected Wenro. A few arrows did miss the shields and strike the individual Vikingars. One hit an iron helmet and bounced harmlessly off, another hit a wealthy Vikingar's chainmail and also failed to cause any injury. Another Iroquois archer got extremely lucky and his arrow passed through the eye aperture of a Viking helmet, burying itself in the eye socket of the hapless Vikingar. The stone arrowhead penetrated the skull and the stricken Vikingar and he immediately dropped, mortally wounded.

As rehearsed ad nauseum, the shield wall reformed around him and kept moving. By now, the Svinfylking had closed with the Iroquois warriors and a hand-to-hand engagement of iron swords against quartz tipped tomahawks and war clubs commenced. The din was overwhelming consisting of the war whoops of the Onondaga and Wenro warriors and the grunts and cries of the wounded of all races. As agreed, the Wenro warriors now dropped the projectile weapons and came from behind the Svinfylking to engage the Iroquois. No quarter was asked for nor given, and the slaughter was intense.

The Viking shields proved their worth absorbing many tomahawk chops and warclub swings. The unprotected Iroquois had nothing to absorb the Vikingar sword blows and many started to fall. The Iroquois warriors didn't lack for bravery and didn't run from the fight. A few of them were able to aim their blows around the Vikingar shields, striking the men themselves. While the Iroquois weapons were tipped with stone, not iron, they were still very effective cutting weapons. While most of the Vikingars had iron helmets, not all did. When a tomahawk or war club would impact a helmet, the iron would deflect the blow. When one hit a Vikingar skull, it wasn't deflected, and that was fatal for more than one Viking.

The Wenro and Vikings developed an effective battle rhythm of the Vikings maintaining their shield wall which the Iroquois were focused on breaking. While the Onondaga were battling the Vikingars, the Wenro would come and strike them from behind. If the Iroquois turned to face the Wenro warrior, the Vikingar would then stab the Iroquois' unprotected side or back. If the Iroquois didn't turn, the Wenro would bury a tomahawk in his back.

After a hard fight that seemed to last forever, but probably lasted no more than fifteen minutes, the Onondaga had lost dozens of warriors killed or maimed. The brave Iroquois finally accepted that they were beaten, and those that could, broke ranks and fled. Neither the

Vikingars nor the Wenro pursued them. The Vikings had no reason to, and the Wenro had other tasks to focus on.

As Olav had explained the scalping practice to Magnus, he was prepared for what he was about to see. Even for the hardened veteran Vikingars, seeing what now happened was noteworthy. The Wenro proceeded to scalp every Iroquois they found, alive or dead.

Seeing that the scalping of the wounded Iroquois he'd witnessed earlier wasn't an anomaly, Magnus asked Olav, "Why don't the Skraelings kill their wounded enemies before they scalp them? And can a man survive a scalping, if his other wounds don't prove fatal?"

"It does seem strange. Let me answer your second question first. Yes, a man can survive a scalping if he doesn't succumb to his other wounds or blood infection. The obsidian knives used by the Skraelings are sharp, but not as sharp as iron. For some reason, when they use them to remove a scalp, it doesn't bleed as much as you'd think. And that is the answer to your first question. The Skraelings prefer a scalped man to survive, as he becomes a walking testament to the prowess of the tribe that scalped him. As long as that man lives, the top of his head will be bone and will never grow hair again. So, every time another Skraeling sees him, they will know what tribe scalped him, and think twice about warring with that tribe. We could learn a few things from these Skraelings."

Now that the fighting was over, Magnus had to assess the casualties the Vikings had sustained. One Vikingar had been struck by an arrow in the eye and the arrowhead had penetrated his eye socket into the frontal lobe of his brain. He was still alive, but other Vikings had to restrain his arms so he wouldn't try and pull the arrow out. Another Viking who was skilled in tending to wounds, was going to try and remove the arrowhead, which would quite possibly kill the wounded man. Another Viking had been struck by a tomahawk in the side of the neck, which had severed a jugular artery, killing him. A third man had been struck by an arrow where his neck met his chest, piercing his windpipe. He was now breathing with horrible gasping and sucking noises and was slowly suffocating to death. Still another had been hit by a warclub on the back of the neck, breaking his spine and killing him. A final Viking who couldn't afford an iron helmet had been struck by an overhead blow by either a tomahawk or warclub, which had split his forehead open and was fatal.

There were three dead and two dying Vikingars. Additionally, several others had arrow wounds that hadn't penetrated a vital organ or an artery, and excluding an infection, should survive. Two more had received warclub blows to their arms that had broken bones and would require setting and splinting. One man took a tomahawk blow to the wrist; it didn't sever the hand, but it may have well as it was only attached by a few ligaments and tendons and would require amputation. Several more had taken glancing blows that would leave noticeable scars but barring the ever-present threat of a blood infection, should heal.

The Wenro's first order of business was scalping the fallen Iroquois, which was done by each specific warrior that had taken out that Iroquois. The Wenro even marked each shaft of their arrows or atlatl spears with the owner's sign. So, when they came across a fallen Onondaga with a spear or arrow in him, they knew which Wenro had earned his scalp. Magnus did notice one instance that a dead Iroquois had not one, but three different arrows in his corpse. Each arrow had a different man's sign on its shaft, and the three Wenro involved were having a heated argument over whose had proved fatal and should therefore get the scalp. It appeared to Magnus that the three might come to blows, but then Saundustee stepped in and de-escalated the situation by deciding on which arrow wound appeared the most lethal.

Saundustee then came over to Olav and had him ask Magnus if the Vikings were going to scalp the Iroquois that they had eliminated. Magnus answered that as scalping wasn't a Viking practice, they were not, and the Wenro were welcome to the scalps. Saundustee was ecstatic upon hearing that, and first had the two warriors that hadn't got the scalp from the thrice pierced Iroquois come up and remove a scalp each. As there were still several more Iroquois felled by obvious Vikingar sword wounds, Saundustee then allocated their scalps to Wenro he felt had done something to earn one, including Olav. Saundustee looked at Olav, pointed to an Iroquois, and said something to Olav. Olav took out his knife, put his knee in the back of the deceased Iroquois, and lifted off his scalp.

He looked at Magnus sheepishly and said, "I'm living amongst the Wenro now and doubt I'll ever go back to the Land of the Norse, so...."

"You've taken a Wenro wife, you might as well take an Onondaga scalp." After all the scalps had been taken, the Wenro proceeded to loot the Iroquois dwellings and bodies.

Most of the valuables in the longhouses had been taken out by the departing women and children, but the Wenro looted anything they thought of value. Saundustee asked Olav if Magnus wished his men to collect any of these spoils of war.

"We still have a long Viking ahead of us, so cannot get too encumbered with extraneous items." After thinking about it for a few moments, he added, "However, I'm sure my men would like to keep some of the warclubs and tomahawks from the fallen Iroquois." Olav spoke briefly to Saundustee who then spoke to the Wenro warriors. Saundustee then said to Olav who told Magnus, "Saundustee would like all of your Vikingars who were on the outside of the Svinfylking to form a line." Magnus responded with, "A handful of those are dead or dying, but all the rest will do as he asks." After the surviving Vikingars formed a line, Saundustee ceremoniously walked down the line, presenting each man either a tomahawk, warclub, or obsidian knife from the vanquished Iroquois. Afterwards, the Wenro went to each Iroquois lodge, and opening a pouch each warrior carried, took out a piece of iron-pyrite and quartz chert. Striking the two together, caused a spark that was used to ignite the wood and thatch huts. Soon the entire village was ablaze and the Wenro were ready to depart.

Magnus was discussing with his men on how they would extricate the Vikingar casualties, as they certainly were not going to leave them for the irate Iroquois. Overhearing this conversation, Olav said, "The easiest method is to make travois."

"What's a travois?"

"A travois consists of a platform or netting mounted on two long poles, lashed in the shape of an elongated triangle; the frame was dragged with the sharply pointed end forward. Sometimes the blunt end of the frame is stabilized by a third pole bound across the two poles. The Skraelings drag the travois by hand, and sometimes fit it with a shoulder harness for more efficient dragging. You all saw the numerous dogs in the Wenro village. Those are also used to drag the travois. A travois can either be loaded by piling goods atop the bare frame and tying them in place, or by first stretching cloth or leather over the frame to hold the load to be dragged."

Magnus had his men pull poles from the huts that hadn't completely burned down, and with Olav overseeing, started to build a travois for each casualty. They tied the fallen Vikingars' shields across the two poles to become the platforms on which the dead and wounded would ride. As several of the wounded had leg injuries that would make walking forty miles a virtual impossibility, extra travois were constructed. Once completed, there were a dozen travois that would carry the casualties, to be pulled in shifts by the roughly sixty able men.

The Wenro had a like number of dead and wounded, that the built travois to carry as well. Once the construction of the travois were complete, and the non-ambulatory passengers were strapped onto each, the journey home began. As before, groups of Wenro marched ahead, on the flanks, and to the rear to prevent a vengeful Iroquois ambush. The Vikings and all the travois moved in the center. Magnus was impressed by how well the travois moved along the trail back to Cayuga territory. By frequently switching out the men pulling the travois, they were able to make good time.

They covered about ten miles before it got dark and made camp. As before, security was placed all around and maintained throughout the night, as Skraelings were more than willing to fight regardless of the time, or the weather. Olav had told Magnus that attacks at night, and in the dead of winter, were not uncommon. They arose before dawn to prepare for the day's journey. The Vikingar who had been wounded in the throat had expired sometime overnight and was now at peace. The Vikingar who'd had the frontal lobe of his brain pierced by the arrowhead was still alive, but wished he wasn't. Due to the fever raging through his body, or possibly the traumatic brain injury he'd received, he had gotten progressively worse throughout the night. By the time dawn broke, he'd gone stark, raving mad. His fellows had to completely tie him down to the shield on the travois, as his incessant trashing made it difficult to pull. The men pulling that travois had to be switched out the most frequently, not due to physical fatigue, but rather the mental exhaustion of hearing their comrade rant and rave.

As the day progressed Magnus began to wonder if he might not have to release the man from his torment, by suffocating him. Fortunately, he didn't have to make that difficult decision, as by mid-afternoon he'd lapsed into a coma. By the time they'd reached the Cayuga village just prior to nightfall, he was also dead.

The Cayuga were excited to see their Wenro allies return victorious, and there was much jubilation amongst all. The Wenro warriors proudly displayed their scalps, and the Cayuga were appropriately impressed. The Wenro were effusive with their praise of the Vikingars fighting ability, and at the obligatory post-battle feast that night, pregnant Cayuga women came to the Vikingars and had them place their hands on their swollen bellies, to impart their warrior strength to their unborn children.

After the feast, the Wenro and Viking warriors, exhausted after walking eighty miles over four days and fighting a battle, fell to sleep. Magnus had asked Olav if the Cayuga would have sentries for security, but Olav told him they weren't needed. When Magnus asked why, Olav pointed to the numerous dogs in the Cayuga village and said that they provided all the security needed. Admiring the dogs' muscular physiques and large teeth, Magnus agreed.

Their sleep was deep, but it wasn't dreamless, as several men were awoken with nightmares of the battle. This primarily effected the new recruits. When they awoke screaming, their veteran comrades next to them told them it was common and would get better over time. Although, the veterans would tell them the next morning that the post-battle nightmares would never stop entirely, only lessen. After rising the next morning, they loaded the two long-ships and proceeded to sail back up the lake to the Wenro village.

The Wenro villagers were thrilled to see them return, although that joy turned to grief for some of the women when they were told that their men were dead. While most villagers were ecstatic, some quickly turned to wailing. Magnus observed that it was no different from when a Viking ship returned from a raid. The families were mainly thrilled to see their provider return alive, but some, after having peered in vain for their men's face, began wailing upon realizing that he was now in Valhalla. As the Cayuga had been, the Wenro were impressed by the number of Onondaga scalps taken, and the woman of each warrior that had one began preparing it for the ceremonial scalp dance.

The scalp dance was a solemn ceremony to the Wenro, and the first step was to prepare the scalps for the dance. The women first dug a hole in the ground and made a fire. Over the fire they dried the scalps until they looked like parchment. The elaborate preparation of the scalps continued after they dried. The Wenro would make hoops out of green tree branches, and then stretched the scalps on the hoops. After that was done, the women painted, and decorated the scalps before finally affixing them to poles. Magnus and the other Vikingars were pleased that all the females performing custodianship of the scalps removed their deerskin dresses and were nude. When then preparations had been satisfactorily completed, all the warriors who had taken the scalps marched gravely one behind the other, around the village, each bearing his wand with its burden of dangling scalps in his hand. The wands were then planted in a circle in the center of the village. By this time, the whole population of the village was crowded around this center of interest.

The warriors who took the scalps are now joined by those who had taken part in the fight, or who belonged to the party which did the fighting, and thus won for themselves the right to participate in the dance, even though they had no scalps. The women of the warriors that had participated in the assault on the Onondaga, also joined in the dancing. Saundustee told Olav that all the Vikingars were invited to join in the scalp dance. Magnus passed the word to his men that if anyone wanted to participate in the Skraeling dance, they were welcome to. Many of them did, but Magnus was more interested in watching from a ring side seat.

All the dancers assembled in a circle around and facing the circle of wands. At a signal, all the dancers joined hands, and commenced a monotonous song and dance, turning slowly about the scalps. As the dance progressed, the dancers loosed their hands, and varied the song by whoops and yells, and the dance by bounds, gestures and brandishing of weapons. In this manner the dancers worked themselves up to a condition of excitement bordering on frenzy.

The eyes of the spectators were trained upon the scalps and dancers as each slayer in turn sprung from the circle, and bounding to his wand, exclaimed in extravagant terms his own prowess, and acted out the taking of the scalps. When the fortunate takers of scalps had all exhausted themselves in self-laudation, other warriors sprung by turns into the circle. Each explained by what unfortunate circumstance he was prevented on this occasion from taking a scalp, and recounted in glowing language his successful prowess on some previous occasion, or what he proposed to do on the next opportunity.

Magnus noted that the dancers and spectators grew wild with excitement. By the time the dance was over, the attendees were little short of insane. Magnus was impressed that this level of mass hysteria was attained with no chemical assistance at all. Olav shared a little of his precious mead with Magnus and his officers, but the Wenro had none. Throughout the evening, the obligatory tobacco pipes were passed around the spectators. Magnus made sure that Dómaldr was observing all of this to include in his saga.

The next morning the funerary rites for the slain Wenro and Vikings took place. The Wenro dead were temporarily buried, in order for the flesh to decompose so the bones could be cleaned for their proper, final funeral.

Norse burial of slain Vikingars varied by the social status of the deceased. If the dead were high ranking, they would be buried in a longship or elaborate burial vault. As none of the Vikingars killed in the battle were high-ranking, the time involved process of constructing burial vaults was not required. These Norsemen would be cremated. While the preparations for the cremation service were being conducted by the dead's comrades, Magnus sought out his Skald, Dómaldr. "In addition to being able to read and write, can you carve on stone?"

Dómaldr thought about it for a few moments and asked, "Do you mean a runestone?" Runestones were a raised stone with a runic inscription used by Nordic peoples to commemorate a noteworthy event or individual. Magnus nodded his head in the affirmative.

"Yes, I was commissioned to carve several runestone inscriptions back home. I can handle a hammer and chisel."

"Good, I want you to find an applicable stone here, to commemorate the seven Vikingars that died battling the Skraelings. We will leave the stone here, so that when other Vikings come to this village, they shall read of our brave comrades deeds."

"I will compose the sentiments to inscribe today, and tomorrow, I will locate a stone to start carving the inscriptions."

The dead were burned in their daily clothes, along with their personal belongings such as amulets and charms. They performed a traditional Viking funeral where the corpses were being burned in an open-air funeral pyre. After the funeral ceremony, they buried the cremated remains in an urn.

After it was completed, Magnus left to go see if anyone had heard anything from Fólki's scouting party. As he neared the edge of the lake where the other two long-ships were tied up, he heard the men making a commotion. He looked in the direction they were pointing and saw Fólki's ship approaching. Magnus stayed on the lakeside to assist in securing the longship once it arrived. Magnus welcomed Fólki back and told him to ensure that his men had everything settled this evening, and he would speak with him tomorrow to learn how the reconnaissance of Niagara had gone.

Chapter Eight

Magnus sat down with Fólki the following morning. "How did your expedition go?"

"It was very informative. We started out on a southerly course on the river near here, which the Wenro also call the Niagara. Soon after entering the mouth of the river, we lost the wind due to the tall trees on the riverbank."

"That is to be expected, I suppose."

"So, we broke out the oars and rowed, and as it was against the current, it was the cause of many complaints."

"Our Vikingars would complain while being buried alive that their clothes are getting dirty."

Fólki grinned and went on, "We rowed for approximately fifteen miles or so. The river is very nearly a quarter mile across for the first ten or so miles, and then begins to narrow to only a couple hundred feet across. It is still passable by drakkars until you reach the whirlpool. Here the narrowed river takes a very sharp turn that results in turbulent swirling of the river that no longship can safely pass."

"So, at this point we rowed our boat to the riverbank and got out. Leaving a handful of men to watch the ship, the rest of us proceeded to walk along the riverbank. The Skraeling trail is well trod, but not wide enough to porter a longship up without cutting down trees alongside it. After walking for about three miles, we reached the Niagara waterfall, and the waters there certainly thunder! Once you pass the waterfall, the longships can be put back in the river. We walked for roughly twenty more miles till we reached another lake. That lake went on for much further than we could see, even by having some of the younger Vikingars climb to the tops of trees to look. So, from the mouth of the river here, it is approximately thirty miles to the other lake, with only about three being unpassable for the long-ships."

Magnus nodded his head. "We'll have to do some axe work for three miles or so. Considering that we can use the felled trees to roll the long-ships on, it will actually work out well."

After spending the morning going through the post reconnaissance debrief with Fólki, Magnus left to go see how Dómaldr's task of carving a runestone was going. Magnus found him looking at a relatively flat piece of rock approximately three feet long, by eighteen inches wide, and six inches deep. It looked to weigh around two-hundred pounds.

"Is that to be the runestone?" asked Magnus."

"Aye. And I spent last night speaking with the dead Vikingars' comrades and composing the inscriptions. Do you wish to hear them?"

Magnus nodded his head and Dómaldr began. "One of the dead Vikingar's brothers is also on this Viking. In his honor I will inscribe:

Nafni raised this stone in memory of Tóki, his brother. He died in the west battling Skraelings.

The next inscriptions will read:

Tosti and Gunnarr raised these stones in memory of Gunnar and Bjôrn, their comrades, who died on a Viking far beyond Vinland. These two valiant men were widely renowned on Viking raids. Hvatarr and Heilgeir raised the stone in memory of Helgi, their father. He travelled far to the west with the Vikings." Faðir had these runes cut in memory of Ôzurr, his kinsmen, who died in the west on a Viking raid. Tosti raised the stone in memory of Gunni, his kinsman-by-marriage, Gunni's fate was met westwards. Bjôrn and Steinfríðr had the stone raised in memory of Gísli. He fell abroad in Magnus's retinue.

After reciting the inscriptions, Dómaldr asked Magnus, "What are your thoughts? Should I make any changes or additions to them?"

Magnus shook his head. "Not at all, they are all well-spoken and heartfelt, and each has meaning for the kin and comrades of the dead. Any Vikingar would be proud to have those runes carved in his honor. How long do you think it will take you to carve them?" Dómaldr thoughtfully scratched his beard then said, "The stone doesn't appear too hard, so I should be able to get almost one inscription carved per day. So, in about a week's time, I should be finished."

"Good, while you carve the runes, the rest of us will prepare for our continued Viking over the Niagara."

Over the next several days, Magnus took stock on the health of his men as they prepared to voyage up the Niagara. Besides the seven dead Vikingars, there were another dozen that had also been wounded by the Iroquois. Of those, five were relatively minor and shouldn't suffer any impediments. Four were more serious and would take some time to heal. The last three were very seriously wounded and would probably never heal completely.

There was always the possibility that infection could set in on any of the twelve. If that happened, the puss would run, and their fever would spike. If a man was stricken by infection, either his body would defeat it, or he would die. Magnus had seen many Vikingars develop infected wounds, particularly when the weather was warm, as it was currently. Magnus was going to have Olav ask Saundustee if it would be all right to leave the seven more seriously wounded back here at the village while the remainder journeyed up the Niagara. When and if they came back, they could retrieve all those who survived. If they didn't return this way, those Vikingars would either live the rest of their lives with the Wenro or join another Viking that stopped here.

After taking stock of his men, Magnus oversaw how the outfitting of the journey was proceeding. They were in the process of trading the Wenro for many ears of corn, beans, pumpkins and other gourds. They still had some salted and dried meat from Vinland and would be able to fish in the river and hunt along its banks to supplement. Many Vikingars had also traded items with the Wenro for tobacco leaves to put in their mouths and chew. They had been introduced to this practice during the raid on the Onondaga, and many Vikingars now swore by the increased alertness, concentration and wakefulness they felt after chewing it.

Magnus also spent time with Baldr and Fólki streamlining the load plan for the three longships, considering the casualties they had taken. Magnus asked Olav to accompany the Viking due to his local knowledge.

Olav pondered it for a few moments and then replied, "I am only familiar with the shoreline of this lake. Fólki has been farther than I have. Even though I speak the Wenro language, it would do you little good once you get beyond that other lake that Fólki saw. I know there are Iroquois speaking tribes around that lake as well, but as you journey south, you'll come to the lands of the Algonquian-speaking Delaware peoples. Their language is little like the tongue of the Iroquois people, and I speak none of it."

"Another reason that I don't wish to go is that my wife and children are here now. The wife and children I once had in the Norse-land are gone. I don't want to undertake a long Viking to unknown lands, where I might never see this family again either."

"I find no fault with your rationale for not wishing to go with us. You're right that we have no idea of where this Viking will end, and when, if ever, we'll return. I couldn't promise you that you'd ever return."

After pausing for a moment, Magnus continued, "As you'll probably be able to understand the Skraelings around the next lake, I would value your presence there very much. Would you be willing to come with us to the other lake, and then turnaround and come back? If you can find a handful of Wenro to accompany you, we could tow your canoes behind our long-ships, and once we were into the lands of the Skraelings around the other lake, you could return here."

"I should be able to find a few Wenro warriors to go along. I will ask Saundustee tonight if this will be all right, and if so, I will see who I can find."

Magnus slapped Olav on the back and said, "Excellent, we will maintain the use of our translator for another fortnight or so."

The next morning Magnus spoke with Olav again. Olav replied, "Saundustee said that the Wenro are currently at peace with the Iroquois tribe called the Erieehronon on the southern shore of that lake, called Erie. I asked him if it were all right for me to journey with you there, taking a few Wernro warriors with me. He said that he has been wanting to send a trading party there to cement the Wenro's alliances with the Erie peoples, this would be the perfect opportunity. So, he is going to send one of his sub-chiefs along on the party, Wáhta. Instead of the three warriors I initially asked to accompany me, he will send nine plus me, so we will fill five canoes."

Elated by the news that they would be able to communicate with the Erie tribes on the next lake, Magnus told his men the good news. After explaining this to his men, Baldr said, "There is another potential translator that might accompany us, if you will allow it. One of my men, Brant, has made a friend among the Wenro."

"Tell me about Brant's friend!"

"Brant met Onatah the first day we arrived here. She's the widow of a Wenro warrior killed by an Iroquois war-party sometime last year. She's the sister of Olav's wife, so already knew some Norse when she met Brant. Her and

Brant have become quite close over the last few weeks, and as she and her husband's only child was stillborn, she wishes to go wherever Brant goes. If she's allowed to join us, she can act as our translator after Olav returns here."

Scratching his beard, Magnus said, "Have Brant come see me."

A short time later, Brant approached and said, "You wish to see me Forungi?" which was the Norse word for leader.

Magnus nodded and said, "Tell me about the lady friend you've made with the Wenro."

"I met Onatah at the feast when we arrived. She is sister of Olav's wife, and so was able to understand some of what we were saying. Her name means 'daughter of the earth' and she is a head shorter than I, and very voluptuous. She has the most beautiful laugh I've ever heard. Looking into her brown eyes is like getting drunk on mead. While I realize that we're on a Viking, and not attending a 'thing' looking for wives, I love her and don't ever wish to leave her."

"I can see that if I don't allow her to come along, you'll be absolutely worthless for the rest of the Viking. I will allow it, but you need to realize some things. The most important is that by allowing you to bring your lover along, I risk morale and cohesion problems amongst the remainder of the crew. They will absolutely be jealous of you, the only Vikingar to have a winsome lass with him. You must be very careful of this. You cannot show obvious signs of affection for Onatah around the other Vikingars. If they see you kissing and snuggling with her, their morale will plummet, and jealousy will shoot like a comet."

"At night, you and Onatah mustn't be overt in your love making. If the other men hear you two giggling, moaning and squealing under your bedroll, I'm likely to have a mutiny on my hands! If your captain tells me that you two are violating these rules, I will separate you and put her on another longship. Once aboard, who knows? She just might find another Vikingar she likes more than you!"

"Do you already have a wife back home that may not appreciate Onatah keeping you company? I ask because if you do, the two of them may not get along when we return."

Brant shook his head. "No, I don't yet have a wife."

"Do you understand what I expect of you and Onatah?"

Brant stood fully erect and loudly answered, "Completely, Forungi."

"Good, now off with you."

While this conversation was transpiring, Dómaldr the skald, came by. Seeing him, Magnus said, "Well Dómaldr, you can now write in my saga that this Viking has become a love boat. Now, tell me, how is the carving going?"

"That is why I came to see you, I just finished the last inscription and wanted to show you the result."

They walked over to view the runestone. Magnus noted that Dómaldr had only carved on the top two feet of the three-foot tall rock, leaving the bottom foot blank. He had then dug a hole in the ground and stood the rock upright in that and filled it. To provide stability, Dómaldr had leaned the rock back slightly and placed a boulder behind it. Magnus had to admit that it was well entrenched and wouldn't be moved without tremendous exertion. The runestone was there to stay for far longer than either of them would live.

Magnus had Baldr and Fólki take a break from their preparations and bring all the men to walk past the runestone and note the inscriptions. After all the Vikingars had observed the memorial to their dead comrades, they were sent to finalize the preparations.

Magnus told Saundustee that they would leave the next morning. He replied that they would have a feast that evening to see them off.

That evening's dinner was a bit more subdued than the previous ones, as both the Wenro and Vikingars knew that it was quite possibly the final goodbye. As always, the obligatory pipes were passed after dinner and smoked before everyone retired for the night.

Chapter Nine

The next morning dawned clear as the Viking and Wenro accompanying them arose to depart. Saying goodbye to the wounded Vikingars remaining behind was the hardest part. Two of the most severely wounded had developed infections and were probably dying. One of the Vikingars who had one forearm bones broken by a warclub blow begged Magnus to be allowed to go with them. The Wenro had done an admirable job of setting and splinting his fracture, and even had wrapped a wet poultice around the arm that would dry and harden to protect the wound. The Wenro medicine man had told them to leave the dried poultice on for more than two months before removing. The Vikingar could use his fingers, and if the bone healed as the medicine man had said it would, he should regain full use of his arm. Therefore, Magnus relented and let the man join them.

While several other of the wounded men seemed to be healing well, none asked permission to go. Magnus observed that was probably due to the Wenro maidens who took care of them. And these maidens were often topless due to the summer heat. Seeing these young women waiting on the wounded Vikingars and tending to their needs, Magnus was surprised that some Vikingars didn't administer self-inflicted injuries to try and remind behind as well!

After the final farewells were said, the party boarded the longships and set sail to the Niagara river. As Fólki had told them, the mouth of the river was wide for quite a way before it began to narrow. When it did, the trees along the riverbanks blocked the wind and out came to oars. Viking oars were deigned to be rowed in unison and were therefor cut to different lengths depending where in the ship they were employed. This was so that the oars wouldn't interfere with each other. Skraelings used paddles in their canoes, which operate somewhat differently than oars. The Wenro were impressed to witness how a boatload of roughly sixty men, seated on benches, worked together to row the boat, all while repeating sing-song rowing chants. The Wenro canoes were tied behind the longships, being towed.

The journey went well, and by the end of the first day, they were at the whirlpool that Fólki had mentioned. The waters here were widely turbulent, and while Magnus felt that it might just be possible to have a longship make it through, it wasn't worth the risk to try. Therefore, they drew their longships ashore, and camped for the night.

The sub-chief that Saundustee had sent along, Wáhta, told Magnus that they were still in Wenro territory. Magnus understood this, but since they had just launched an attack on an Iroquois tribe, he wasn't taking any chances. He posted security along the riverbank to assure that vengeful Onondaga wouldn't bother them. The men would switch out during the night to reduce fatigue. All the Vikingars knew that Magnus woke frequently at night, and when he did, he would usually arise and walk the lines. If he found a Vikingar asleep while on watch, it would be unpleasant, to say the least.

The first and only infraction of sleeping on post during this Viking had resulted in a public punishment the next day. Magnus had the offending Vikingar stripped of his shirt and then tied face-first to the long-ship's dragonhead prow. Then, the man's immediate superior took his leather sword belt and whipped the offender's naked back until it was covered in welts. After the public flogging, the offender was cut down, told to dress, and informed that if he was caught sleeping on post again, the punishment would be a blood eagle.

Magnus knew that he wouldn't really enact a blood eagle on one of his men for sleeping on-duty, but he didn't need to. The thorough flogging and the threat were enough to ensure that sleeping on post never happened twice in the same Viking. After a whipping, Magnus would make sure that the offender was placed on night security again in the near future. And when he was, Magnus would make it a point to get up and walk the lines. He had yet to encounter a repeat offender. It was amazing what a public flogging and fear of a horrible death can accomplish regarding attention to duty.

When dawn arose' Magnus, Baldr and Fólki, Olav and Wáhta walked along the riverbank to reach Niagara Falls. It was less than three miles from where they beached their boats below the whirlpool to the falls. They heard the falls long before they came around the bend in the river and saw them. The Norse Land had many waterfalls that Magnus had seen, but none like this. Magnus noticed that there were actually three waterfalls, separated by two islands. He estimated that the three falls combined were nearly four thousand feet across and dropped approximately two hundred feet to the river below. And how they thundered!

Witnessing them in person, Magnus fully understood why the Skraeling word Niagara meant 'thundering waters." Through Olav, Wáhta asked Magnus if his homeland had waterfalls such as this?

"We have many waterfalls in the land of the Norse, as our land is very mountainous. And there are some very tall waterfalls there, such as one called Mardalsfossen, where the river falls over several tiers. Its overall height is taller than this, but the river feeding it is not nearly so wide. In all my travels, I've never seen this much water going over a waterfall."

After the party admired the waterfall's power, they got down to business discussing how to get the longships up the river. Magnus asked Fólki what he'd discovered on his reconnaissance.

"We went through one set of rapids before we got to the whirlpool. There is another set of rapids we'd have to go through before the falls if we put our ships back in the river after the whirlpool. And obviously we will have to take our ships out again once we reach the falls."

Baldr said, "Your crew are strong rowers, I feel confident that you can make it up the falls in your ship."

Fólki gave Baldr a sardonic look. "Oh, why couldn't your mother's intelligent son come on this Viking?"

Magnus interrupted the playful banter. "Fólki, we had to overcome some minor rapids as far as we got. How is the river once you get past these falls? Any other places that would require us to portage the ships?"

"After the falls, the river is bisected by two islands, one of which is quite large. The river's flow there seems somewhat gentler, but I did notice some other significant rapids before we reach the next lake. So, I can't promise that once we get past these falls, we won't have to haul the ships out again to bypass rapids."

Magnus shrugged his shoulders. "Well, it looks like our men are going to get some exercise navigating this river." After admiring the falls one last time, the party turned around and headed back.

Upon reaching the main party, it was late afternoon and Magnus had Fólki and Baldr bring their subordinate leaders to him. Once they were assembled, Magnus said, "It is about three miles to the falls. There is another set of rapids in-between the whirlpool and falls, so I see no use putting the ships back in the river to pull them out again so soon. So, we will need to portage the ships for three miles till we get them above the falls. As you can see, the trail along the riverbank isn't wide enough for the long-ships, so we will have to cut trees to widen it. We will lay them in front of the boats to act as rollers to pull the ships on. We will divide the party in two groups that will rotate each day. One to cut down and lay the trees, and one to push/pull the ships. We will assemble parties to hunt and fish as needed. Once we get past the falls, we can put the boats back in the river, but may have to pull them out again to bypass rapids. We will start tomorrow." After checking for questions, Magnus sent them back to the ships to prepare for the morrow. As a parting thought, he told them to use whetstones on their axes, as they would need to be sharp.

After redistributing the ship's crews prior to departure, each ship was carrying approximately seventy men, including Wenro passengers. Baldr and Fólki's ships were known as Skeids that were just under a hundred feet in length with thirty rowing benches. One Vikingar set on each side of the bench and rowed. Each also had a single mast holding a woolen sail measuring approximately 3000 square feet. With their large sails and sixty oarsmen each, the skeids could achieve speeds of around fifteen miles an hour under sail with the men rowing. Magnus's flagship, called a drakkar, was about ten feet longer and more ornate with an intricately carved dragon head prow and five more rowing benches for seventy oarsmen. All three ships were approximately twelve feet wide and had a draught of slightly over three feet. Their shallow draughts allowed them to go very far up rivers and to easily beach themselves. The relatively light construction of each long-ship meant that they only weighed about 20,000 pounds.

That comparatively light weight and large crews were going to pay dividends now. Even though they couldn't sail up a waterfall, they could be carried around it. The Vikingars acting as axe-men cut down the trees on the riverbank until a roughly fifteen-foot-wide path had been cleared. After the trees were cut, the axe-men trimmed any branches preventing the trees from lying flat. The trees were then laid perpendicular across the path. The long-ships were manhandled on top of the logs, which now served as rollers. With half the boat's crew taking hold of ropes tied to the prow of the ship and pulling while the other half pushed from the sides and back, the longships were pulled several hundred yards per day.

Although they were still in friendly territory, Magnus had each ship post at night a pair of Vikings for security. They walked around the sleeping Vikingars not only to prevent a surprise attack from any hostile Skraelings, but also to prevent thievery from fellow shipmates. It pained Magnus to admit that Vikingars would steal from their comrades, but he had been around too long to pretend it wasn't true. The Vikings even had a saying about this internecine larceny, "There is only one Vikingar thief, everyone else is just trying to get their things back."

The night passed uneventfully and the next morning the men arose to start their work. The Dane axes they carried were primarily for fighting but were very effective at cutting trees as well. The trees consisted primarily of various oaks, maples, willows, birches and evergreens. Magnus couldn't help but notice that these trees would provide excellent timber for constructing ships. The riverbank echoed with the sounds of axes biting into trees, and the trees crashing down. The Vikingars soon developed a rhythm, and Magnus had the axe-men and boat-men switch places in the afternoon. Progress went well, even though the direction of travel was uphill. By the end of the day, all three boats had moved a couple hundred yards and now that the process was established, should move even further the following days.

Once the rhythm was solidified, Magnus's Viking was able to move approximately five hundred yards a day along the riverbank. The biggest complaint of most of the men was the blisters that developed on their hands from their time with the axes. They soon learned that wrapping cloth around their hands while swinging the axes helped reduce the friction.

As there wasn't a tremendous amount about to be recorded in his saga, Magnus had his skald participate in the cutting and dragging. While most of men changed places every day, some of the Vikingars seemed to relish cutting timber and preferred doing that to manhandling the longships. As there were plenty of Vikingars who didn't enjoy repetitively swinging a Dane axe at a tree, it worked out well. Magnus was happy to let individuals remain as axe men if they wished, providing that forward momentum continued.

Magnus noticed that the Vikingars that wanted to stay on the axes all had broad shoulders and backs. And he knew that by the time they had passed the falls, their shoulders and backs would be even broader. The Wenro didn't have axes, so they tried to help with moving the ships. While their willingness to work was certainly appreciated, Magnus soon realized there was something else they could do. The Wenro were very skilled hunters and fishermen. As Magnus didn't wish his men to consume their stockpiled food before it was absolutely necessary, he asked the Wenro to procure food instead of push boats.

And they did! Everyday, they sent out parties to hunt and fish. They would return with deer, elk, bison, moose, beaver and numerous species of fish to feed the party. At the end of each long day of cutting trees and moving ships, the Vikingars knew that they would dine well on nature's bounty thanks to the Wenro.

After ten days of work, the Vikingars had moved from the whirlpool to the falls. After a couple more days, they had moved the longships above the falls to a point they could be placed back into the river. Subsequent to almost two weeks of very heavy manual labor, every Vikingar was happy to sit on the rowing benches of the longships again. While rowing was certainly physically demanding, at least it could be done while sitting down! As the wind blew predominantly from the north, and their direction of travel was south, their long-ships' sails were able to take the wind and little rowing was necessary. From where they put the ships back in the river above the falls, it was only about fifteen miles to Lake Erie.

They hit rapids at another point along the river but were able to disembark crewmen ashore holding lines tied to the ships. The crewmen ashore held onto the ropes and stabilized the boats as they traversed the rapids. Once through the rapids, the crewmen reembarked and the long-ships continued their journey. With the wind at their backs filling their sails, they made good time and by the end of one day had reached the head of Lake Erie. As they neared it, Magnus had the Wenro untie their canoes and paddle ahead of them to let the Erie know they were coming. He shouldn't have bothered, Erie Skraelings had been monitoring them for days and knew exactly where they were. The Wenro hunting parties had even encountered Erie parties and had in-depth conversations with them. It was laughable for Magnus to think that there were any Skraelings in this part of Vinland that weren't aware of exactly who and where he was, always. Being six-foot-tall, blonde and blue eyed with a heavy beard, Magnus didn't exactly blend in with the locals. By the time they reached the first village on Lake Erie, an Erie welcoming party way waiting. As Saundustee had told him, the Wenro and Erie were on good terms, so they were greeted with much joy. And as Magnus had grown accustomed to, a feast was prepared in their honor.

The celebratory feast had similar components to those Magnus had experienced with the Wenro. There was venison and fish to eat, as well as the 'three sisters' of beans, squash and corn. By now, the Vikingars had developed a taste for these items, and consumed them with gusto. And as with the Wenro feasts, there was singing and dancing. The Erie weren't on good terms with the Iroquois either, and were very excited to hear about the combined Wenro and Viking assault on the Iroquois village. As several of the Wenro warriors traveling with them were also in the attack, they were asked by the Erie to perform in a descriptive dance. They agreed, so all those in attendance at the feast saw them dance and sing about their tales of valor. The Vikings were also asked to perform, and while Magnus declined, several of the younger Vikingars took the opportunity to do so. The dancing Vikingars had all seen how the Wenro danced at a post-battle feast, so they had an example to mimic.

A part of the dance was the warrior reciting tales of his glorious deeds in a sing-song, rhythmic chant. Since none of the dancing Vikingars spoke the Skraeling tongue, they couldn't chant anything the Wenro or Erie would understand. No matter, they instead chanted in Norse. Olav told them what types of discourses the Skraeling warriors sang and danced about, so they did their best to imitate that. Magnus was impressed by the Vikingars dancing about in the Erie longhouse, and singing chants about Odin, the god of war, and how he ruled in Valhalla, where all brave Viking warriors went after death in battle.

One of the Vikingars took it even further, and sang about Odin's two black ravens, Huginn and Muninn, that flew forth daily to gather tidings of events all over the world. Upon hearing this song, Magnus chuckled to himself and thought that Huginn and Muninn must surely have told Odin about Magnus's Viking by now.

While the Vikingars were singing and dancing, Magnus sought out his Skald. "Dómaldr, make sure you include this in my saga. It could set a new entertainment trend back home." Dómaldr nodded his head emphatically and laughed out loud. Magnus made a mental note that while he could imagine Vikingars having consumed multiple cups of mead dancing and singing like this, not a drop of mead had been drunk here.

Whilst the young Vikings were jumping about in their best imitation of Skraeling dancers, the ceremonial pipe bowls were passed about. Magnus had become very enamored by this affectation and never missed an opportunity to take a puff when the pipe was passed to him. Although he had to be careful when he took a pull. If he did it too fast, he would inhale the smoke with the resultant cough of a tobacco neophyte.

As the dancing and smoking continued, Magnus said to Olav, "What was that flat tailed animal with the thick fur that the Wenro brought us to eat?"

"Ah, those are the bjorr. The Wenro call them beaver, named after another Skraeling tribe to the north. They appear to be very similar to the bjorr that used to be trapped by our grandsires back home but are now scarce."

Magnus nodded his head. "I thought it looked familiar. Bjorr are now so rare and sought after that the fur-pelt can only be afforded by a prince or jarl." After pulling on his beard for a moment, he said, "Are the bjorr, or beaver, relatively common here?"

"Yes, they are hunted for food and furs, but there is so much fur bearing game here that they are not nearly as valuable as they are back home. They Skraelings do use the furs for clothing, but their tales are more sought after as a food delicacy. And the Skraeling women use them to entice men!"

Not believing that he'd heard Olav correctly, Magnus gave him an inquisitive look. "Huh?"

"The women take the oil from the scent gland underneath the beaver's tail and rub it on their bodies, thinking that it incites a man's lust and desire for her."

Now thoroughly confused, Magnus could only stammer, "Why in Odin's name do they think smelling like a beaver would make a man randy?"

"Seems ridiculous, does it not? The Skraelings believe that as beaver and other animals such as muskrat, use their scent glands to attract mates, so those same glands can also attract men." Noticing the incredulous look on Magnus's face, Olav simply held up his hand and said, "Jarl, please go back to enjoying the tobacco and festivities."

Magnus did exactly that and didn't even notice that Olav then wandered off. Olav wasn't wandering about aimlessly; he was on a mission. He went to Honniasont's table, the Erie chief, and explained to him that he had told the Viking chief about women's use of musk scent as a perfume, but that Magnus didn't believe it. So, Olav asked if Honniasont could find a maiden that had some musk scent, so Magnus could smell it in action.

The Erie chief smiled and said that he had just the maiden in mind, his oldest daughter. He called for her and explained to her what she was to do. She went to her lodge, got out her carefully guarded musk oil, and rubbed some on her neck and wrists. She then went with Olav to the table where Magnus sat. When they arrived, Olav said to Magnus, "Forungi, this is the daughter of the Erie chief and she would like to give you a hug by way of welcome."

Not one to turn down a hug by an attractive young woman, Magnus stood up and opened his arms. The teenage girl grabbed Magnus by the back of the head and pulled his face into her neck. When she did, Magnus's nose was right where she had dabbed the musk. Unconsciously inhaling it, Magnus was immediately aroused. Not understanding his state of arousal, he let the lass go and she returned to her father's table.

Noting the look of confusion on Magnus's face as he watched the girl walk away, Olav asked, "Everything all right Jarl, you look perplexed?" Magnus gave a noticeable shake of his head, wiped a hand over his face and answered, "No, everything's fine, I was just thinking."

"Thinking what?"

"I'm really not sure what or why."

"I can tell you exactly what and why!"

"And how would you know?"

"When that winsome lass hugged you, you were immediately aroused, and you have no idea why."

Magnus nodded his head. "She's certainly a pretty girl, but she is by no means the first attractive girl I've hugged. And all she did was give me a friendly hug, nothing more. Why would I feel so stirred by her?"

"Because you're not so different from a horny male beaver or muskrat. I asked Honniasont's daughter to put on some musk oil and let you smell it."

"Well, maybe there is something to this after all! How do the Skraelings hunt beavers?"

"They use several methods including include deadfalls, snares, nets, bows and arrows, spears and clubs. In winter the beaver is captured by means of nets formed of thin, hardened thongs of deer-hide, the meshes several inches square. Holes are cut made in the ice, about twenty feet apart with an ice-chisel. The ends of the net are then passed from one hole to another by means of a long pole placed beneath the ice; and stretched by means of stones attached to the lower corners. The beaver lodge is then disturbed; and they make a break towards their refuges and are entangled and captured."

"I have seen deadfalls being used. Those are comprised of baited tree logs. When the beaver approaches to eat it, a log falls on the animal, killing it. This method is mostly used during warm months when there is little snow. Sometimes a pole fence is erected beside the beaver lodge entry so the animal can't escape. The Skraelings then bore a hole in the ice on top of its house so that when the beaver comes out through the only opening, the hole, the hunter kills it with a spear."

"Additionally, Snares loaded with stone weights are placed in shallow water close to beaver dams and then coated with the musk oil as bait. In early spring, the hunter makes holes near the beaver lodge and places poplar or willow branches over the hole as bait and returns later to see if the beaver has eaten it. If so, he hides under a blanket and waits for it to come back to eat. He then spears the beaver. In winter, when the snow is high, hunters will break down a lodge and use bow and arrow, club or spear as the beavers try to escape. The Wenro use their canoes to raid beaver lodges in spring. Families of beavers build many lodges, so the lodges are linked by a trap line along which a hunter will walk over a period of days to inspect for trapped beaver."

An idea was forming in Magnus's mind. The Vikingars that signed on for his expedition knew that its primary focus was to be exploration, not wealth. However, that didn't mean that they would be averse to earning some coinage. Vikings could be launched for various reasons, and most dealt with turning a profit. In order to find Vikingar volunteers to undertake a voyage, it helped if they thought there was a good chance of their earning wealth. Affluence in the Viking world was frequently obtained via raiding. When the Vikings raided a village, they would take anything worth money that could be loaded onto a Viking long-ship. These items obviously included precious metals and jewels. Portable artwork, if it could be recognized, would also be taken. And always, thralls. Slavery was one of the major economic engines in Viking society, and roughly twenty percent of the population of Scandinavia was enthralled or enslaved. And even though most wealthy karls and jarls had already purchased their needed thralls, there was always a need for more. As might be expected, the working conditions for most thralls were less than ideal. Therefore, thralls were frequently injured or even killed. A seriously injured or dead thrall couldn't work, so a new one must be purchased.

And there were other markets for Viking thralls. Vikingars had been sailing down the Atlantic into the Mediterranean for hundreds of years by Magnus's time. They spent so much time there, they eventually colonized Southern Italy and the Island of Sicily. The reason they were there so frequently, besides escaping harsh Scandinavian winters, was that was where two of their biggest and wealthiest customers were. The Eastern Roman, or Byzantine, and Islamic Fatimid Caliphate empires. Both empires had extensive wealth and voracious demands for thralls. As Western Europe's thrall market was relatively saturated by now, the Vikingars went east. They knew that by taking their newly acquired thralls into the Mediterranean, they would surely be able to sell them for good money. The Island of Sicily had been taken over from the Muslims by the Norsemen several decades before Magnus's birth, but both cultures still interfaced openly there along with the Byzantines, so that was the place to sell thralls.

Magnus smiled to himself as he imagined telling his Vikingars that they were going to start capturing Skraelings as thralls. He laughed as he visualized the looks on his men's faces as he told them they were about to embark on something that would surely get them all killed. His roughly two-hundred men were going to start trying to enslave a population of who-knows-how-many war-like Skraelings. What could possibly go wrong?! Magnus softly chuckled as he thought about his men's reaction to that mission statement.

Mutinies were rare among Vikings, but if there was ever a justified mutiny, that would be it! Fortunately, there was one other money-making option for the Vikingars amongst the Skraeling that hopefully wouldn't result in them losing their scalps. Besides selling plundered wealth and thralls, the other sought-after product from Northern Europe was furs. Eurasian Beavers, which were very similar to the ones hunted by the Skraelings, were now nearly extinct, much sought after and expensive.

If Magnus could set up a winter encampment amongst good beaver hunting grounds, he didn't see any reason that each of his men couldn't get several dozen beaver pelts to bring back to Europe. Since the Eurasian Beavers' near extinction, the most common furs harvested in Northern Europe were now weasels, martens, the occasional fox, and particularly squirrels. In the lands of the Viking Rus, squirrel fur was so valuable that it was used as a currency. Magnus had heard tell that land-rents were actually paid in several squirrel pelts in Rus-land.

Magnus imagined the sheer lust on the faces of the Karls and Jarls as Magnus's Vikingars disembarked the longships holding aloft luxuriant beaver pelts. In addition to the pelts, Magnus was now a believer that the musky scent glands of animals like the beaver were an aphrodisiac for humans. Magnus made a mental note to ask the Skraelings how they harvested that scent from the animals and processed it into oil that could be dabbed on a woman's body.

Magnus's Viking would not only bring back expensive pelts to sell, but perfume as well. Magnus rubbed his hands together thinking of this addition to his Saga.

By the end of the Erie welcome feast, Magnus had come up with a solid plan for his Vikingars to make money on their return to Europe, with furs and perfume. Now that Olav had given Magnus a thorough description of how the Skraeling hunted beaver, Magnus asked him another question. "How do the Skraelings harvest the scent glands of beaver?"

Olav raised his hands in supplication and said, "I have watched the Skraelings remove the scent glands, or sacs, from underneath the animal's tails, but besides observing that they did it very carefully so as to not rupture the sacs, I can't give you a useful description." Olav then thought for several seconds before adding, "Let me ask chief Honniasont which of his men is the best beaver trapper, and then I will bring that man over and ask him questions about it."

Magnus watched Olav walk to the chief's table and ask to speak to him. Olav was invited to sit down with Honniasont, and the obligatory pipes were brought out and lit up. Olav and the chief became very engrossed in a thoroughly lengthy conversation. As Magnus watched, he became convinced that it had to be about more than beaver scent glands. The two seemed to talk for hours and with a full stomach making him drowsy, Magnus put his head on his arms and dozed off at the table.

He awoke when he felt someone approaching him. He sat up as Olav finally returned from the Honniasont's table. "By Thor's Hammer," said Magnus, "did the chief take you out to run a trap-line to further your beaver harvesting knowledge?"

Olav smiled as he sat down at the table. "Jarl, please forgive my lengthy absence, that conversation about beaver scent glands ended up being anything but."

"Oh, really? What?"

"I asked the chief about who his best beaver trapper was. He wanted to know why I cared, and I went in depth explaining our desire to learn how to harvest beaver. Honniasont, who is a highly intelligent and inquisitive man, asked me many questions about why harvesting beaver was so important to us. I explained to him that the beaver was nearly extinct back home, and therefore very valuable, hence our desire to take pelts back with us when we return from our Viking."

"The chief replied that while the Erie could certainly teach we Vikingars how to efficiently skin and harvest the scent glands of a beaver, hunting them was an artform that took years to get good at. He said that if we wanted to master the art of beaver trapping ourselves, then we'd better be prepared to be the Erie's guests for several years."

"I was afraid of that. Your explanation of hunting techniques sounded pretty straightforward, but I felt that the implementation of such techniques would require a demanding learning process."

Olav smiled. "The chief's conversation then turned to how he could remedy that."

Magnus gave Olav and inquisitive look. "Is that so?"

Olav nodded his head. "Of course, we will have to do something in return."

Understanding now why Olav and the chief were speaking so long, Magnus asked, "Does Honniasont wish us to attack an Iroquois village like we did with the Wenro?"

"No, we won't have to fight anything except the streambeds leading to the lake."

"What in Odin's name are you talking about?"

"As I said, the chief is a very smart man. And as all Skraelings are, he is fascinated by our iron weapons. He had learned about our smelting iron from bog ore up in Vinland and asked questions about that. I told him that yes, ever since Leif Erickson first landed there decades ago, we've been harvesting iron ore from the bogs there to smelt into iron. He had me explain how the process worked, from finding the ore in the bog, to smelting it into iron, to hammering it into weapons or tools."

"He listened intently and then had an Erie Brave go retrieve something from his longhouse. The Skraeling returned with a fist-sized piece of rock. The chief said that a Viking that came through Erie territory several years ago had found it on the riverbank of one of the streams that leads into the lake. The Viking that found it gave it to the chief and told him that was bog ore, suitable for making iron. Honniasont handed it to me and asked if that was true. I told him that I thought so, but I wasn't a blacksmith, so couldn't be certain. I then told him that we did have a trained blacksmith on the Viking and I had them fetch Håkon over from another table. I gave the rock to Håkon who looked at it and said that it definitely was bog ore, and it seemed to have a high iron content.

"The chief was thrilled and said he'd shown it to all the Erie and told them that if they came across any of these to pick them up and bring them to the village. Over the past few years, they had collected several wicker baskets of rocks. Honniasont took Håkon over to the long house to look at the rocks. Håkon gave the baskets a once over and told me that while some had little or no usable iron content, many rocks had a decent amount that was suitable for smelting."

"I passed this information onto the chief, and he was overjoyed. Honniasont then made a business proposal. He stated that if we allowed Håkon to set up a blacksmith forge in the village and begin rendering the collected bog ore into iron for tools and weapons, Honniasont would send out the Erie on hunting parties to collect beaver pelts and musk sacs, and he would also send out word to neighboring tribes that the Erie were in the market to trade for any available beaver pelts. Honniasont asked me if I thought you would be agreeable to this, and I told him I would certainly ask."

Magnus thought the proposal over for several moments. "Go find Håkon and send him to me. If he tells me that this is feasible, then I'll have you fetch Dómaldr so he can add trading iron for beaver to my saga."

When Håkon arrived, Magnus motioned him to sit and explained what he was thinking. "I know that when you agreed to come on this Viking, working as a blacksmith was the last thing you thought would happen."

Håkon said nothing in reply but raised his eyebrows inquisitively.

Magnus went on, "As a way for all the Vikingars to make money, I approached the Erie chief to see if he would be willing to let us harvest beaver pelts to take back. The Erie chief said that if we would smelt the bog ore he showed you into iron, he would have his braves harvest all the beaver we wanted."

"That sounds like in order for our Viking to earn wealth, my skin will again be getting black with soot!"

Magnus gave a big smile and clapped his hands. "Excellent, now Håkon I need you to explain to me the process of smelting ore."

"This will be a lengthy explanation; I recommend we share a Skraeling tobacco pipe during it."

'That sounds like a capital idea" said Magnus and he sent Olav to ask the Erie for a pipe.

Chapter Ten

Several minutes later Olav returned with a pipe, extra
tobacco, and a glowing ember. Magnus lit the pipe, took a
pull on it, and passed it to Håkon. He likewise took a pull
and passed it to Olav, who passed it on to Magnus when he
finished his drag.

After taking a puff, Magnus said to Håkon, "Educate me
on what we need to do to make an iron forge."

After drawing and holding smoke in his mouth for
several seconds before exhaling, Håkon began." First, let
me say that as my blacksmith experience is from
Norseland and Vinland, some of the particulars required
here will surely be different."

"No doubt."

"Streams often carry iron chunks from nearby
mountains. Which is why the Skraelings have found it by
the riverbanks. When the iron nodules are carried into a
bog by the river, their presence can be detected on the
surface by the iridescent oily film they leave on the water,
another sure sign of bog iron. We call that iron slick a
jarnbrák. When a layer of peat in the bog is cut and pulled
back using turf knives, pea sized nodules of bog iron can be
found and harvested. It's been my experience, although the
iron nodules are reasonably pure, there aren't many of
them. They are, however, a renewable resource. About
once each generation, the same bog can be re-harvested."

"The Erie will be happy to learn that."

Håkon smiled and went on, "In some regions, such as the land of the Rus, iron rock rather than bog iron, is the raw material for smelting. The ore is often in the form of "red earth" called rauði by the Rus, a powdery ocher. Regardless of the source, the raw materials are first roasted to drive off moisture. The roasting also serves to "crack" the surface of the iron ore, making it more porous so that the heat in the smelting furnace can enter and react with the iron more easily. Once the dry nodules or ore are in hand, smelting can begin."

"The smelting operation is performed in a bloomery furnace, which is a small clay or clay-lined shaft. The furnaces are roughly circular, and about three feet tall and one foot in diameter. The clay used is a mixture of sand, fiber, clay, and water. The fiber is often horse dung, in which the undigested hay provided the fiber. This mix has the needed structural properties to contain the smelting materials, as well as appropriate insulating properties. The walls must radiate enough heat to keep the inside surface from melting into the slag during the smelt."

"The furnace can be built around a tapered wooden form, or simply by building it up from an earthen base. First tying off the outside with rope to prevent sagging, and filling the inside with a sand/ash mixture to draw water out of the clay."

Magnus interrupted, "I have yet to see horses, cows, goats, sheep, or any other domesticated animals amongst the Skraelings to produce dung. Olav, am I mistaken?"

"The only domesticated animals I'm aware of here are dogs and the occasional turkey. Neither of which consume hay."

Håkon held up his hands. "No worries, dung isn't required, I'm sure the Erie can produce dried plant material for fiber."

After the pipe was refilled and lit, Håkon continued his lecture, "As the clay dries, the wooden form or the sand/ash mixture is removed, and the drying is completed with a gentle wood fire inside the furnace. Smelting furnaces are also made from stacked turf, with a shaft in the center, lined with a thin layer of clay. There are several ways to make the furnaces, depending on the materials at hand."

'To begin the smelting operation, a fire is started inside the furnace with a natural draft, to prevent the shock from rapid heating damaging the furnace. One warmed, an air blast is supplied through the side of the furnace with a bellows, and the bore of the furnace is filled with charcoal."

Passing the pipe to Olav, Magnus said, "Besides furnaces, we'll need to manufacture several bellows. My skald should be here to write all this down!"

"No worries Jarl, after years of blacksmithing, I can recite this in my sleep."

"The next step is forcing air into the furnace through the tuyere, via a vent on the side of the furnace. We use a tuyere made of copper. The placement of the tuyere is a critical parameter in the success of these furnaces. The air blown in is adjusted to control the burn rate, and ore and charcoal are regularly added to the top of the furnace. Inside the furnace, the temperature is hottest at the bottom of the furnace near the iron. This atmosphere creates a gas that somehow helps draw impurities from the iron in the rock, leaving just the iron. The temperature in the furnace is coolest at the top and hottest near the bottom. Different reactions occur in the different temperature zones of the furnace. Throughout the smelting process, additional fuel and ore are added at the top of the furnace. The process is tended to constantly, adjusting the fuel, ore, and air via bellows to optimize the results. The smelting operation takes many hours, which explains why blacksmiths are coated in black ash by the time it's complete."

"I knew that being a skilled smith required special knowledge, but now I'm gaining a new appreciation."

Håkon continued. "Slag is both the waste product of the smelting process, and an essential element to the smelting process. Liquid slag at the bottom of the furnace is contained in a bowl formed by solidified slag. Iron formed in the upper part of the furnace drops down and collects in the slag bowl. If the liquid slag rises to a high enough level to block the air from the tuyere, the iron making process is impacted."

"The level of the slag can be monitored, both by the sound of the air passing through the tuyere, and by visually watching the process through the bore of the tuyere from the outside end. If the slag level rises too high, a door in the bottom of the furnace, can be opened and liquid slag drained out. The molten liquid slag flows like water. This process continues for a very long time, many hours over the better part of a day, and requires constant attending to maintain optimal conditions inside the furnace. Fuel, air, ore, and slag all require constant attention."

"When the smelting process is complete, a section of the lower furnace is removed, and a frothy iron sponge-like material called a blástrjárn, or bloom, is levered free of the furnace walls. The bloom is a mixture of low-carbon iron, slag, and charcoal. The surrounding slag and charcoal are knocked off. Immediately after removing from the furnace, the remaining material is hammered with sledges to consolidate the material. This work is best done while the bloom retains the heat from the smelting process. A wooden log anvil is often used, since the heat of the bloom burns a depression in the wood, helping to hold the bloom in position as it is worked. The bloom is refined by folding it, which serves to homogenize the material and to drive out the impurities, such as slag. This folding process is repeated multiple times to create cleaner, purer material. The end-result is a billet of malleable iron, ready to be forged to fabricate the required tools or weapons."

After taking another drag from the communal pipe, Håkon went on, "Now let's discuss what the blacksmith shop contains. There is usually a stone-lined cistern in the center of the floor for holding water. Next to the cistern is the hearth, filled with charcoal and soot. A stone lined channel runs in the floor from the hearth to the outside serving as an air channel for the fire. Even with a relatively small fire, it is possible to heat treat large items by continually moving the workpiece in the fire. Two bellows working alternately blow into the fire through a soapstone bellows shield, which keeps the fire from reaching and igniting the wood and leather bellows".

"I know that among out Vikingars, there are several who worked as journeyman blacksmiths at one time or another. Let me draft them to help me in the forge, to work the bellows and so forth. Jarl, we will need considerable assistance from the Erie to make this process happen."

"If the Erie chief wants us to manufacture iron weapons for him, I'm sure he'll be willing to help as needed."

"Good, the Erie will need to help us construct the clay furnaces, gather more bog iron, and provide me apprentices that I can teach to be blacksmiths after we're gone."

Taking a final pull on the pipe, Magnus said, "Håkon, you are a wealth of knowledge concerning blacksmithing. I want you to find Dómaldr and have him write down what we need from the Erie to make our 'bog iron for beaver' venture a reality. Dómaldr will then give me that list, and I will speak to Honniasont so we can start the process."

Next morning, Dómaldr approached Magnus with a list written on a deer skin. Magnus, who was fairly literate in Old Norse, took the skin and looked at it. "What did you use for ink?"

"I used some of the paint the Wenro decorate their lodges with."

Magnus nodded his head and began reading the list, asking questions when he came across a word he didn't recognize. After he made sure that he understood the contents of the list, Magnus found Olav. Showing him the list, he said, "How are you at reading?"

"Not very good, Forungi."

"No matter, I will read the list of what we need from the Erie and you will tell Honniasont.".

Chapter Eleven

Magnus and Olav met with the Erie Chief and his sub-chiefs in his longhouse. Through Olav, Magnus told Honniasont that the Viking blacksmith would indeed be able to turn the bog ore rocks into iron for the Erie, provided that the Erie were willing to help. Honniasont and the sub-chiefs were ecstatic and said that they would provide any help necessary. Magnus, reading from the deer skin list, told them that the first order of business was to create the forges necessary to smelt the iron. Håkon would teach the Erie how to make a forge so that they could do so after the Viking departed.

Honniasont asked Olav to wait until they gathered some of the maidens who would be doing most of this work. Magnus took this a step further by suggesting that they all reconvene in the open, where Håkon could demonstrate the construction of a stacked turf furnace.

Magnus and Olav left the longhouse and went to find Håkon. Magnus explained to him about the upcoming demonstration. Håkon agreed that it was the best idea and went to get the tools necessary to cut the appropriate turf and then picked out a well-suited area adjacent to the village.

After the Erie assembled, Håkon began the demonstration with Olav explaining it to them step-by-step. As Olav spoke, Håkon demonstrated that the first step was cutting and rolling out layers of sod. Once each layer of sod was unrolled, Håkon cut out the center of it for the fire chamber. He then lined the center of the chamber, with a thin lining of clay mixed with sand.

Håkon said that dried plant material could be used as fiber. "To ensure that the clay lining will stick to the turf, it is wise to lay some clay between turf layers that is firmly attached to the clay wall lining." Håkon then created a tunnel in the lower turf layers to a clay door in the side of the shaft lining to use for extraction and tapping. Next, he laid in a shaft between the turf layers and clay lining for the tuyere to be inserted and laid the final layers of turf on the iron furnace.

After setting a clay door in the shaft lining at the bottom, Håkon got some wood to build a drying fire inside the furnace. Through Olav, Håkon told the assembled Erie that the drying fire would need to burn for a while, and that they could all come back the next morning.

Most Erie left, but a few remained behind to ask questions. While the drying fire was going, Håkon spent some time making rudimentary bellows out of wood and leather. After tending the fire and constructing bellows, Håkon told Magnus that the furnace was complete and the next day he would get some bog ore and smelt some iron.

Next morning, all the interested parties reconvened at the furnace with Håkon, who had slept there after much tweaking through the night. Håkon and two black-smith experienced Vikingars lit a fire inside the furnace and used the bellows to make sure it was stoked. After the fire was ready, Håkon took bog ore pellets and started inserting them into the furnace.

As the furnace got hot and the turf on the outside dried, the smiths occasionally poured water on it, so the turf wouldn't ignite. They would also periodically look down the tuyere shaft to see how the smelt was proceeding.

Everything that Håkon did, Olav described to the Erie, so that they both heard and watched. At times, Håkon would take a long stick to re-open the turf tunnel as the sod settled. This allowed him to tap the slag. Håkon explained that the heated slag was draining to the bottom of the furnace. After several hours, Håkon stopped adding bog ore and let the furnace burn down.

Håkon and his apprentice smiths then got a small tree with the branches cut off to serve as a pole. Using the pole inserted into the top of the furnace, the smiths smashed the bloom free from the walls of the furnace so that it could be extracted. Using an iron hammer from the ship, he compacted the bloom on top of a wooden anvil.

After compacting the bloom, and dipping it in water to cool, Håkon passed the fist-sized chunk of raw iron around to the Erie and told them that next day he would show them how to make into arrowheads from the iron. After finishing the day's lesson, the assembly was adjourned.

After the demonstration ended, Magnus asked Håkon, "I knew that you could smelt the bog ore into iron, but can you really show the Skraelings how to turn it into useable weapons?"

"I believe that the Erie will give us many more beaver pelts if I show them how to hammer the iron into useful items. When I came on this Viking, I knew that my blacksmith skills would probably be required for things such as ship repairs. So, I brought most of my tools with me. Tomorrow, I will heat the bloom to red hot, and then fold it several times. After a few hours, the end-result will be a billet of malleable iron, ready to be forged to produce tools or weapons. I will have that stage complete by the end of the day, and on the following say, I will forge several arrow heads for them. When I do, I will ask for several Erie volunteers who want to learn how to be blacksmiths, so I can teach them what to do after we leave."

Magnus was pleased at how this was proceeding and believed that the Erie Chief was as well.

The next morning, the instruction started again. Magnus intended to ask Honniasont how to select a few Erie that Håkon could train, but Honniasont was way ahead of him. Several Erie spiritualists or Shamans filled in the front row. The Erie considered the knowledge of making iron to be nearly mystical, which is the reason Honniasont told the Shamans that they were to become the tribe's iron workers.

The Shamans held a revered place in Skraeling society, and forging iron was likewise considered awe inspiring, so the Shamans seemed eager to learn.

Håkon began by heating the furnace and then the bloom. Once the bloom was red-hot, he began the folding process, and repeated it several times until he had created a billet of iron pure enough to be turned into arrowheads. Olav explained all of this while Håkon worked. Once the iron billet was considered refined enough, Håkon heated it one last time so he could shave off arrowhead sized chunks. When complete, Håkon had almost a dozen chunks of iron pure enough for arrowheads.

After the iron chunks were cool, Håkon passed them around to the assembled Erie and told them that each of these would be a sharp arrowhead when he was done. After collecting the iron chunks, Håkon put his hammer by the anvil and got everything ready.

While preparing, Håkon said, "There are two main ways of attaching arrowheads, socketed or tanged. Generally, the socketed type is more common in the lands of the Gaels, and the tanged is more common in our land. The socketed arrowheads take much longer and require considerably more skill to make. As the Skraeling stone arrowheads are all affixed to the arrow shafts using tangs and sinew, I see no reason to change that with the iron ones."

"As far as the shape of the arrowhead, there are probably two that are best for the Skraelings. One is known as the Leaf, as that is what is resembles. This is probably the earliest form of arrowhead, and it can be used both for hunting and for war. There is also the Shouldered type. Just like the leaf shaped heads, these are multipurpose heads that have a more angular shape to them. There is a third arrowhead type called a Bodkin, used purely for war to split open chainmail shirts, but less efficient at killing unarmored creatures. They are narrow and come to a point without having any sort of shoulder. As the Erie don't have any enemies that wear chainmail, I see no reason for us to forge those."

Magnus agreed.

Still laying his tools out, Håkon said to Magnus, "Let's talk about the proposed tang for the arrowheads."

Not being a blacksmith himself, Magnus was completely in the listening mode and motioned for Håkon to continue.

"An arrow with a slender conical tang is slightly more difficult to forge than the flat tang, but much easier than the full socket. It also uses the least amount of iron per arrow, which will also be a consideration for our Erie friends. The tip of the wooden shaft is prepared by drilling or burning out a small hole of a size to fit the tang. As the head's tang is conical, mounting a head means only tapping it into place. I will show, and Olav will tell them, that the shoulder area between the tang base and the head's shaft be must be as close to flat and square as possible. On impact, this flat area evenly distributes the impact force over the surface of the wooden shaft, resulting in the least potential damage to the shaft itself. In reality, because of the conical shape of the tang, the arrowhead is still likely to simply pull free out of the shaft on any attempt at extraction. So, when the Erie are on the warpath, and one of these arrows impact Iroquois flesh, most likely the arrowhead will be left behind, increasing the wound. Another benefit for the Erie in a battle since the arrowheads will remain in whatever they hit so they can't be easily picked up and used against the Erie."

Håkon indicated to Magnus that he was ready to commence the arrowhead production demonstration. Olav went around to the Erie and made sure that all the future metal working Shamans were in attendance. Håkon first fired up the forge to heat the iron billets to a bright orange and placed one on the anvil. He used his hammer and the tongs to hold the first iron billet as he hammered it down to roughly a quarter inch square. Håkon continued to hammer on the iron billet, repositioning it occasionally with the tongs. The process of hammering out one shouldered arrowhead with a conical tang took a bit of time for Håkon to complete.

After finishing one arrowhead to his satisfaction, Håkon took out a couple of whetstones and began to sharpen the arrowhead. After running the arrowhead over the two whetstones, with Olav explaining why, Håkon was satisfied with the arrowheads blade. He passed the complete arrowhead around to the Erie to see the finished product.

Håkon and Magnus were pleased to see that one of the Erie ran his finger too hard over the blade, resulting in him gasping in pain as he held up a finger dripping blood. Everyone in attendance took note of this and understood how fine a blade iron could hold.

Håkon told Olav to have the Shaman ironworkers to approach the forge so they could work the iron themselves. Håkon picked one Shaman to be the first student, and with Olav interpreting as Håkon demonstrated, he had the Erie trainee first heat the billet in the forge, and then begin to hammer it. Håkon made it a point to have other Erie pupils, work the bellows of the forge, to keep the fires stoked. Håkon took his job of teaching the Erie Shamans seriously, and after one demonstrated an understanding of iron forging, he would have another take over.

Meals were brought for everyone in attendance, and by darkness, several Erie students had taken turns learning how to hammer a shouldered arrowhead from an iron billet, and then sharpen it with a whetstone. At the end of the day, both Magnus and Håkon were pleased with the Skraelings performance. Becoming a skilled blacksmith took much longer than a day, but Magnus felt that with Håkon tutoring the Shamans for the next several weeks as the Erie collected beaver belts for the Vikingars to take back with them, the Viking would leave them as competent iron workers.

That night the Erie held a feast to celebrate the fact that they were being ushered into the iron-age, under the tutelage of the Vikingars. Magnus made sure that Dómaldr was seated next to him during the feast to give him a synopsis of what he had recorded for the saga.

Later, Honniasont, the Erie chief told Magnus through Olav, told him that the Shaman students had told him all about the day's lessons. Honniasont was incredibly pleased and told Magnus that he had divided all available Erie into two parties. One party to hunt beaver, and the other to collect bog ore from the local waterways. One of the Shaman had given Honniasont a sharpened arrowhead, and throughout the conversation he kept gently fondling it. Honniasont also made a point to tell Magnus that the Erie were also collecting the musk glands from the beaver that they were harvesting.

After the feast, the next few weeks settled into a routine. Håkon continued to teach the Erie the finer points of iron smelting and implement manufacturing. As Honniasont had promised, the Erie that were not students at the forge, went afield to either gather bog ore or to harvest beaver. As the majority of the Vikingars were not assisting Håkon at the forge, Magnus had them accompany the Erie hunting beaver, or gathering ore.

After the hunting and bog ore parties diminished the ore and beaver near the village, they then started venturing farther afield. Honniasont had also sent out word to the neighboring friendly tribes, that the Erie would pay well for all beaver pelts. Magnus accompanied several beaver hunting parties and was impressed by their hunting skills. The Vikingars practiced fur bearing animal harvesting back in Scandinavia, but the Skraelings took it to a new level of expertise. In between accompanying hunting parties, Magnus observed the techniques the Erie used to preserve the pelts.

Firstly, the excess fat and flesh of the beaver were scraped off with a sharp, yet blunt tipped bone or stone tool. The skin was then pegged out flat on the ground or it was laid over a slanted log to provide a hard, stable surface with to work on. Next, they dried the skin under the sun until it was stiff to prevent the fur from slipping from the pelt.

Magnus was impressed by the ways the Skraelings used whatever they had at hand. After they harvested the beaver, they would crack open its skull to retrieve the brains. They would soak the skin of the animal in brain solution mixed with water. The beaver pelts were kept overnight in this solution. Magnus noted that other organs such as the spinal cord, liver, bone marrow, fat, as well as vegetable matter were sometimes used as well, but brains seemed to be the most important ingredient. Olav told Magnus this was to promoted softness and pliability in the pelt.

After the soak was complete, the next step involved stretching and working the skin until it was completely dry and soft. The beaver pelts were rubbed over a stick, a log, or a certain rock. The brains and other softening materials were scraped and rubbed off during this process until the skin was velvety soft and flexible. Magnus was impressed by the luxuriant softness of the beaver skins at this point, but there was still one more final step. The Erie took the pelts and smoked them, making them easier to soften after they got wet. As a bonus, insects were less likely to investigate a smoked skin.

Smoking was accomplished by hanging the skin over a slowly smoldering fire in order to absorb the fumes. The skins were hung up in buildings called smoke houses, which were designed especially for this process. Since they would be taking their beaver pelts in their open long-ships across the Atlantic, it was guaranteed that they would get wet during transit. At first Magnus thought that the smokey smell might lower the pelts value back home, but he soon learned it would add to their value.

Magnus's Viking spent the winter in the Erie village as the iron smelting and beaver harvesting progressed. By the end of the winter, the Erie Shaman's iron working skills had progressed to the point that Håkon and his Vikingar blacksmith assistants at the forge were doing no physical labor there themselves, just answering the occasional questions and providing refinements through Olav. By this point, dozens of shouldered arrowheads had been produced, and Håkon had even expended the extra iron ore to manufacture a handful of tomahawk axe heads for Honniasont and the Erie sub-chiefs.

The Erie had also found multiple suitable rocks to serve as various grained whetstones, and Magnus noticed that they took pride in challenging each other to come up with the sharpest blade. The Erie were no longer plucking out their hair with bone tweezers to create a mohawk but were now using sharp iron blades to shave the sides of their heads. The beaver harvesting increased over that winter as the beaver were somewhat easier to hunt with the streams and rivers iced over. The Erie braves brought back a steady supply of beaver skins that the maidens worked on to turn into soft, opulent pelts that would be highly desirable back in Scandinavia.

The Erie were also conscious about the Vikingars' desire to harvest the musk sacs of the animals. They would extract the glands when they skinned the animals and tie-them-up in a plant leaf for the musk oil to be extracted later.

Their bog ore search parties had been hard at work as well, and now that Håkon was only serving in a supervisory role at the Forge, he had the time to inspect the collected ore from the bogs and streams, to select the ones that had useful iron content. Through his tutelage, by the end of winter, the Erie had become adroit at finding, smelting and manufacturing iron tools. Magnus made sure that Dómaldr, was recording all that transpired for the saga.

Magnus also ensured that Dómaldr noted the numbers of beaver pelts that the Erie gave them, so that they could be distributed to his men equitably. By the end of the winter, the Erie had harvested as well as traded with neighboring tribes, nearly five hundred beaver pelts.

Magnus calculated that he and the ship's captains were to get several of the most luxuriant pelts each. The members of the Viking that had done noteworthy work, including Olav, Dómaldr and Håkon as well as a few others, would receive multiple pelts each.

Speaking to his captains, Baldr and Fólki, Magnus said, "I have allocated two dozen pelts for myself and to others that have proven indispensable on this Viking. Approximately a third will be for my ship's crewmen. The rest, I will divide in two even halves and give to you to divide amongst your crews as you see fit. You will each receive approximately one hundred sixty pelts. How you wish to allocate them is up to you, but make sure that each Vikingar receives at least one."

Magnus also distributed the accumulated leaf-wrapped musk sacks, after explaining to Baldr and Fólki that the Skraeling maidens used the oil as a perfume to excite their menfolk. "I didn't believe it, but it actually works."

They were both as incredulous as Magnus had been, so he had Olav find a willing maiden to demonstrate the musk's potency. Olav procured two attractive young Erie lasses to demonstrate. They applied musk oil and made sure to rub Baldr and Fólki's noses where they put it. Both Baldr and Fólki were clearly aroused by the maidens and their musk oil dabbed bodies, and they thereafter believed in the authenticity of musk oil's amorous effects.

As the winter turned to spring, Magnus and his captains knew that it was time to prepare for the long journey home. The Vikingars acting as the ship's quartermasters began procuring provisions of smoked meat to be consumed whenever fish couldn't be caught. They also acquired squash, corn and beans to bring as well, as all three would keep for extended periods before going bad. Baldr and Fólki also spent time going over their skeids, making sure that they were ship-shape. One component of this was determining where the valuable beaver pelts would be stored for the long return journey. The three ship captains decided to keep all the pelts consolidated near where they slept on the ships, so that the Vikingars wouldn't steal them from each other. Once they arrived back in Norse-land, they would distribute them. After several weeks of preparation during the waning winter months, everything was ready for the arduous return trip.

Chapter Twelve

After Olav told Honniasont that it was time to depart, the chief said that he would throw a farewell feast. The feast was the most extravagant one the Vikingars had yet witnessed in Vinland. There were succulent meats, fishes, beans, corn and gourds. There was singing and dancing that some of the Vikingars joined in on. Several of the Vikingars had become romantically involved with Erie maidens over the last few months, and during the feast, Fólki approached Magnus, with two of his men in tow.

"Jarl, two of my men have a question that I believe they should ask you personally." Raising his eyebrows, Magnus looked at the two and motioned for them to speak. One of the young men nervously stepped forward and stammered, "Forungi, my friend and I have a request of you." Magnus's ice blue eyes bore inquisitively into the two as he beckoned them to continue. "We have both fallen in love with Erie maidens who desire to return with us to the Norse-land. Both girls have asked for and received permission from Honniasont, and when we asked Fólki if they could come along, he said we must get your permission."

Magnus took a good long draw on the pipe that had been given to him during the feast as he considered the men's request. Finally, he asked, "Will these be your frille," which was the Old Norse word for concubines, "or do you intend on marrying them upon our return?"

Almost in unison, both men answered, "We wish to marry them."

Magnus rubbed his beard. "Will these be your first wives, or are there others back home?"

"These will be the first for both of us."

"That is for the best. Often first wives don't take kindly to their husbands adding additional ones." Magnus looked at Fólki and asked him, "Are you comfortable with the two maidens embarking on your ship for the sail home?"

Fólki nodded. "I've told both Vikingars that during the day, the two maidens can be near them while we sail. However, at night the girls will sleep on top of the beaver belts near my quarters, so that some of the men's randy crewmates don't decide and try to cuddle up to them. I'm fine with the girls being on my vessel, especially as it will give us all something nice to look at. However, I won't allow them to be the cause of any jealous fights aboard my ship. If that happens, both girls will have to ride the rest of the way on Baldr's ship. Either that, or swim home."

Feeling that Fólki was comfortable with what was to transpire, Magnus finally said, "Well, I already let one of Baldr's men bring a Wenro maiden along, so I might as well let you bring a couple of Erie girls. Fólki, you'll need to do one final thing before we depart. I want you to re-name your vessel after the goddess of Love, Freya."

After looking intently at Magnus to determine if he was joking, Fólki finally said, "Jarl, it will take a long time for you to let me live this one down won't it?"

"Aye! When we're both in Valhalla, I'll still be having fun at your expense over this."

Later during the feast, Honniasont approached Magnus with Olav in tow. Olav said, "Chief Honniasont has something he wants to give you for the return trip."

Honniasont handed Magnus an oiled deerskin pouch. Magnus took the pouch and carefully opened it up, finding it full of seeds and beans of various types.

"Jarl, Honniasont has noticed how we have enjoyed eating the beans, corn and gourds and smoking the tobacco while we've been here. So, he had the Erie maidens select beans and seeds from their best growing crops, to take back with you. He also wants to present you with something else."

Honniasont stepped in front of Olav holding two more deerskin pouches. He opened the larger one and showed Magnus that it contained a large amount of dried tobacco ready to be put in pipe bowls. Honniasont spoke briefly to Olav who then stated, "Honniasont says that the deerskin pouch is thoroughly oiled and should keep your tobacco dry during your journey."

Honniasont then unwrapped the next parcel showing that it contained two beautifully wrought ceremonial pipes. One made of red pipestone and one carved from a greenish-blue, bluestone.

After handing them to Magnus, Honniasont spoke to Olav who then translated, "He says that the red one was carved from stone indigenous to this area, but that the blue one comes from a Skraeling tribe that lives in mountains that lie a many days journey south. He wants you to accept these gifts from the Erie people, and hopes that when you smoke Erie tobacco from these pipes, that you will have fond memories of your time here."

Magnus bowed his head in thanks and told Olav, "Tell Chief Honniasont thank you very much and please ask him to wait here while I retrieve a gift for him."

Magnus walked quickly to his ship and rummaged through his items. Finding what he was looking for, he returned to the feast. Once there he unwrapped a short sword and made a display of presenting it to Honniasont. Magnus them told Olav, "Tell him that this sword is made by the Ulfberht family of sword makers, and it is among the most highly sought after in my land." Everyone in the room looked admiringly at the beautifully wrought and inlaid steel blade. "It is an incredibly strong sword, worthy of a chief such as he."

Honniasont was almost in tears after receiving it and held it aloft as he let out an admiring war whoop.

The next morning dawned clear as the Vikingars said their final goodbyes to their Erie friends. As the longships rowed away from the shore, many Erie canoes did as well, several rowed by Erie braves, whose sisters were passengers in the canoes. They kept alongside the longships for quite a way, with the maidens shouting to the Vikingars to hurry back as soon as possible, and the Vikingars calling out how much they loved the girls. Seeing all this transpire, Magnus felt very confident that many of these Vikingars would be begging him to undertake a return Viking here, as quickly as it could be arranged.

The longships had a good wind out of the north, which was almost directly on their port beam. This wind filled their sails, and quickly the oars were shipped, and they left their Erie friends behind. Magnus knew that if the fair wind held, that they would reach the end of the lake by this time tomorrow.

The wind did hold throughout the day and night, and by morning, they had reached the northeastern lakeshore, where the river proceeded to the Falls.

At the mouth of the river, they lost the fair wind due to the trees on either side. Out came the oars and as the flow of the river was going with them this time, it carried their ships along nicely. The current was moving so quickly, that the men rowing just let the Vikingars serving as the ships' coxswains steer to keep the ships in the middle of the river. By early that afternoon, they had neared the waterfalls. Close to the falls, the current of the river picked up so much that the Vikingars had to row vigorously to get their ships to the riverbank so that they wouldn't go over the falls.

After beaching their boats, Magnus had his men prepare to haul the ships along the trails they had cut last year. As their direction of their travel was going slightly downhill, gravity would ease movement this time. Magnus was happy to see that while a few of the logs they had placed as rollers on the trail last year were gone, presumably taken by Skraelings for use as firewood or building lodges, most were still in place. And while the forest had begun its inexorable march toward the river to reclaim what had been cut last year, the growth on the trail was only saplings, and would pose no obstacle to the Vikingars.

Magnus didn't need to divide the men into two groups as there was no need to fall trees. All hands turned to for moving the longships down the trail. As before, half the crew would push each ship while the other half pulled on ropes affixed to the boat's stem.

Magnus watched as the dragon head prows bobbed as they rolled along the trail bed of logs. He doubted this had ever happened here before and wondered if it ever would again. The boats moved down the trail almost at a man's walking pace. In fact, once they came abreast of the waterfall, the trail's downslope was so steep, they had to use the ropes in a block and tackle arrangement around trees on the trail's edge to prevent the ships from accelerating and plummeting into the river. If that had happened, the ship would have gone over the waterfall before it could be stopped and would have been dashed into a thousand pieces by the nearly two-hundred-foot drop.

They made the journey from where they took the ships out of the water above the falls to just past the whirlpool some distance beneath the falls. Magnus estimated this to be approximately four miles, and as they arrived at dusk of the same day that they reached the mouth of the river, he reckoned that they had made nearly one mile an hour portaging the boats along the trail. Considering that coming up the trail last year, they were doing good to make one mile a day, Magnus was very pleased by their progress.

They bivouacked for the night just downstream of the whirlpool, and Magnus posted security. Even though they were in two friendly tribes' territory, the Erie and Wenro, Magnus didn't take a chance that there wasn't any vengeful Iroquois lurking nearby. And as each of the three boats had nearly two hundred beaver pelts stowed away onboard, he didn't put it past some of his Vikingars to try and liberate some for themselves.

Magnus ensured that each ship had alternating pairs of men always awake through the night for local security. He also organized a roving patrol of two men to walk around all three ships. After ensuring a workable security plan was in place, Magnus had the crews eat and turn in for the night. And as always, Magnus woke at several times throughout the night to ensure that all the security elements were awake and alert. The threats of a whipping and Blood Eagle was still working, and all were vigilant.

Chapter Thirteen

The next morning, everyone breakfasted on dried meat and loaded the ships. They had about ten more miles to make the Wenro village, but once again the current was in their favor and the oars were primarily for steering. The Viking ships exited out of the river and into the lake where the Wenro village sat. The longships arrived at the village and tied up. The Wenro had been aware of the Viking's approach and were awaiting them. Their chief, Saundustee was there on the lake shore, as was Olav's wife and children.

There was a joyous reunion, and everyone embraced warmly. The wounded Vikingars that had remained at the Wenro village to recuperate were there as well. Magnus noted that of the two with severe infections, one had died and had been buried by the Wenro. Saundustee had Olav ask Magnus if he wished the Wenro to disinter the bones so the Viking could take them home?

Magnus thanked Saundustee but replied, "The Vikingar fought and died for his Wenro comrades, so his bones should remain with them forever." After everyone said their helloes, Saundustee pulled Olav aside and talked to him for several minutes, afterwards, Olav came over to Magnus and told him, "Saundustee has prepared a communal feast for this evening and says that he will have something to give you at that time."

"Tell him thank you and I look forward to the evening's festivities." As the ships' crews worked to verify that everything was still ship-shape, Magnus approached Håkon. and said, "Did you save some arrowheads and iron blades like I asked?"

"Aye Jarl, I kept over a dozen arrowheads and two tomahawk blades."

"Good. Are they sharp?"

"They are, but I will run a whetstone over them again anyway."

"Excellent. Bring them with you to the feast this evening."

As the sun set to the west, the Wenro feast commenced. There was more of the same delicious venison and fish, beans, roasted corn and gourds. Olav even broke out some of his carefully guarded mead. There was frenzied singing and dancing, most of it retelling the battle against the Onondaga the previous year.

As they had at the Erie feast, many of the young Vikingars joined in the feverish dances pantomiming their valorous deeds against the Iroquois. Magnus took out one of the pipes given to him by the Erie Chief, filled the bowl and lit it. After ensuring it was lit, he passed it to Saundustee, who pulled from it admiringly. Saundustee asked Olav where it came from, and after Olav explained about it being a gift from the Erie Chief, Saundustee said it was now time for the Wenro to show their thanks to the Vikingars for fighting with them last year.

After the chief quieted everyone in the long house, he made a proclamation that Olav translated, "Last year, these brave men accompanied our braves on an attack on the Onondaga village. They fought alongside of us, and several were wounded and killed alongside of us. Together, we bested numerous Onondaga Braves, which the Iroquois scalps hanging on our lodge poles clearly demonstrate. When these men then journeyed over the Niagara to visit our friends the Erie, we heard that beaver pelts were a very valuable commodity for them. So, to show our appreciation for your valorous deeds, we harvested many beaver pelts over the winter that we wish you to take."

With that, Saundustee motioned for several Wenro maidens to step forward and present the collected pelts. Magnus immediately saw that they were as perfectly preserved and tanned as were the ones the Erie had provided. Their fur was soft and luxuriant, and each was going to fetch an astronomical price back home.

Magnus chuckled to himself as he realized that all the various wealthy nobles and royalty in Europe were going to be dressed in his Viking's beaver fur after their return. He also noted that it wasn't just a few pelts they gave him, but somewhere nearing a hundred.

After accepting the beaver pelts and indicating his appreciation, Magnus motioned for Håkon to hand him the deerskin parcel they had discussed. Upon receiving it, Magnus looked to Olav and told him to translate the following, "These beaver furs are beautiful and will make every Vikingar here very wealthy upon our return. As a token of our appreciation, I have some things I would like to give to you."

Magnus unwrapped the deerskin and took out the iron arrowheads. Presenting them to Saundustee, he said, "These arrowheads are made of iron and will be sharper than any made of flint. I hope that they will provide you much meat for your families and defense for your village."

Then unwrapping the two iron tomahawk heads, Magnus presented them to Saundustee. "I hope when you wield these tomahawks against your enemies, that you will fondly remember your Viking allies."

As a final parting gift, Magnus handed Saundustee the best whetstone they had found, and said, "This stone will keep your iron weapons sharp, and Håkon will show you how to use it."

Saundustee proudly showed the iron trophies to all the Wenro as they admiringly walked by the table. After they had all trooped by, Magnus turned once more to Saundustee. "We showed the Erie how to produce these iron tools from the iron pellets found in your creeks and rivers. I asked Honniasont if he would be willing to show you how to do so, and he answered that he will share that knowledge with his friends the Wenro."

After the feast was complete, the Vikingars returned to the shoreline to rest in preparation for their return voyage. A few of the wounded men had made love connections with Wenro maidens that tended them. One of those approached Magnus after the feast. He was accompanied by Olav and they stood in front of Magnus." Jarl' said the man, "May I speak to you?"

Magnus looked at them both and nodded his assent. "While I recovered from my wound over the winter, I fell in love with a Wenro lass, and we made love several times."

Magnus looked hard at the man. "Are you telling me this to boast about your sexual prowess?"

The young man looked sheepishly at the ground and stammered in reply, "No, Jarl, I now have a son who was born a couple of months ago."

Magnus was at a loss for words hearing that and could only think to reply, "Congratulations Vikingar!"

"Thank you, Jarl. And that is what I wish to speak to you about. I have now fathered a child, and I don't feel right leaving it behind. He even has my cleft chin and green eyes. I am respectfully asking if I can remain behind in this village, with my woman and child?"

Magnus looked at Olav and asked, "Your thoughts?"

Olav scratched his beard and answered, "The Wenro are happy to let him stay, and the girl's family is willing to let him live with them and marry the lass. I will keep an eye on his acclimatization and will teach him the Wenro language."

Magnus nodded his head and asked, "Baldr is your captain, correct?"

"Aye, Jarl."

"Go get him and bring him here."

The man ran off and shortly returned with Baldr. Magnus looked at them both and said, "Baldr, your man here has fathered a child with a Skraeling maiden and wishes to remain with them. What say you?"

Baldr smiled as he replied, "I wasn't shocked to hear it, the way he and the maiden acted around each other while she tended him, it was obvious."

"Can you do without him on our journey home, and are you comfortable in letting him remain behind?"

"Aye Jarl, he's a good sailor but not one that I can't live without. And if we force him to accompany us, he'd be longing so for his woman and child, that he would be more of a hinderance."

Magnus looked at the young man and Olav. "Very well then. Get your gear off the ship, say goodbye to your comrades, and go home to your woman and child."

After sending the man off, Magnus took the time to take count of the beaver pelts given them by the Wenro. These totaled ninety pelts, which made the allocation easy. He divided the pelts into three even piles, and then called for his captains, Baldr and Fólki. Once they arrived, Magnus pointed at the piles and said, "Each of you take a pile to add to ship's allocation. How much will this add to your total number of pelts?"

After quickly counting his pile, it was Baldr who answered, "These will make my total number of pelts be almost a hundred and ninety!"

"After your losses you each have about sixty crewmen, do you not?"

Baldr said, "I currently have exactly sixty-four crewmen."

It was now Fólki's turn to answer, "I started this Viking with sixty-eight crewmen, but lost three."

"I now have seventy-three," Magnus said. For the three of us, that gives a grand total of two hundred and five each. That will be almost three beaver pelts per man. As I said before, allocate the pelts however you deem appropriate, but ensure each man receives at least one."

Baldr rubbed his hands together as he answered, "I am going to save thirty pelts to give my ten bravest warriors and best sailors. Another handful for myself. The remaining pelts will be divided equitably amongst my crew, which will give every man at least two."

Both Fólki and Magnus said they would do roughly the same and Magnus added, "Only the wealthiest men can afford to buy beaver pelts. The two pelts each our Vikingars will have to sell, will earn them some serious coinage. And don't forget the musk sacs. I'm not sure how best to market those, but as we all know, they are a very effective aphrodisiac."

Baldr said, "I'm way ahead of you on that Forungi! When we get back, I will attend the first Thing that is organized. I will bring my two wives with me and we will establish a booth. I will have my gorgeous wives dab the musk oil on their necks and invite the Jarls and Karls in attendance to smell it. When they do, they will be instantly aroused, and want to purchase it for their wives!"

Magnus laughed as Fólki said, "Baldr, you're wasting your talents as a Vikingar, you need to venture to Paris and become a perfume salesman."

The next morning the Vikingars loaded their ships and departed the Wenro village They sailed east towards the mouth of the river that would lead to the ocean. As on the previous lake, the wind was out of the northwest and moved them along smartly. By the morning of the next day, they had transited the entire lake and were at the mouth of the river. The trees on the riverbanks blocked much of the wind, so the vessels had to break out their oars. Using oars augmented by the wind, the longships moved from dawn till dusk, when they would beach on the riverbank for the night.

As before, Magnus emplaced security around the ships at night and they had no problems. After several days, the ships reached the bay leading to the ocean. As they were now free of the trees blocking the wind, the boats shipped their oars and transitioned back to solely sail power. It took the long-ships three days to sail from the mouth of the river to Vinland. As they approached Vinland from the west, the setting sun was at their backs as they pulled in on the evening of the third day. There was another Viking in the bay consisting of two smaller Karvi boats.

Magnus's Viking beached their ships and got out to stretch their legs. The settlement looked much as they remembered, had the same number of dwellings and apparently a similar number of permanent residents, most of whom were conducting business with the Vikingars with the Karvi ships. After making sure that his three ships were safely beached, Magnus walked to the village hetman's house to pay his respects.

As his eyes became adjusted to the dim candlelight inside the longhouse, Magnus saw the Hetman talking to another Vikingar." Ahhh Magnus, back from beyond Vinland, alive and well!" said the Hetman."

"Aye, I am."

The Hetman stood up and motioned for Magnus to join them at the table." Magnus, may I introduce Ketill, he is the captain of the Karvi ships Viking anchored in the bay."

As the two men grasped wrists, Magnus said, "Funny, your nose doesn't look flat."

All three men laughed at Magnus's reference to Ketill Björnsson, nicknamed Flatnose, who was a Norse leader in the Gaelic Isles a few hundred years before.

They sat down, and the Hetman continued, "Ketill has journeyed here from Normandy, in the lands of the Franks." Hearing this, Magnus stated, "So, it was your grandsires who besieged and sacked Paris!"

Ketill chuckled." "Aye, my ancestors were with Ragnar when he took his one hundred twenty longships and 5,000 men up the Seine River and paid his respects to the Frankish King."

"I doubt that the Frankish King enjoyed Ragnar's sightseeing visit very much."

"Well, since Ragnar captured more than a hundred of their knights and hung them by their necks on an island in the river, I can understand why the Frankish King didn't enjoy our visit."

"I didn't know that had been part of the sack of Paris."

"Ragnar's saga states that the Frankish King divided his army in half to defend Paris. And placed one half on each bank of the Seine. Ragnar attacked and defeated the half on one riverbank and took more than a hundred captured knights to an island offshore of Paris, built crude scaffolds, and hung them all. He did this as a sacrifice to Odin, and to let the Franks know what awaited them if they offered more resistance."

"Did that end the Frankish resistance?"

'They offered a bit more of a fight, but couldn't mount an effective defense of Paris, so we took it."

Magnus's ears perked up as he heard this last bit of information.

"I have always wondered why Paris isn't still a Viking held city?"

"The answer to that is simple, 7,000 livres of gold and silver."

Magnus's eyes widened as he asked, "What on earth is a livre?"

"The livre is the currency of the Kingdom of the Franks. They are cast either in gold or silver. To get my ancestors to depart Paris, King Charles the Bald gave them 7,000."

"All of solid gold or silver? How much did that weigh?"

"So much it took several cargo ships for the return to Denmark."

"I can understand why your ancestors stayed in the lands of the Franks!"

"They frequently raided up the Seine for the next several decades, until finally the new Frankish king, Charles the Simple, concluded an agreement with the Viking king Rollo officially granting him the territory of the lower Seine."

"Did you inherit any of the gold and silver?"

"Nary a one, which is why I'm sailing a Karvi across to Vinland!"

The Hetman asked Magnus, "How well did Håkon serve you?"

"Amazingly well, we couldn't have accomplished everything we did without him." Magnus then went into detail describing the iron for beaver arrangement that Håkon played such an important role in.

Both the Hetman and Ketill were amazed by the tale, and Ketill asked, "Do you think if I sail my Karvi into the lake you spoke of, the Wenro would welcome me?"

"Without a doubt. We left on very good terms. A word of warning though, we Vikingars are not on good terms with the Iroquois Skraelings who also live along the lake. If you blunder into one of their villages, it will go badly for you and your crew. And even if you somehow survived, your scalp wouldn't remain on you!"

Seeing that Ketill had zero understanding of what he said, Magnus went in depth to explain the process of scalping.

"The thought of my scalp ending up on some Iroquois' lodge pole does put a damper on the excitement about journeying to your lake!"

Magnus thought for a moment before he replied. "Because of the Iroquois threat, I don't recommend you sailing into the lake unescorted. However, several of my men fell in love with Wenro maidens, and one even fathered a child with one and remained there. I imagine that I can find at least one volunteer that will wish to accompany you to the village. He will know where the Onondaga are, so you can avoid them."

Ketill smiled. "I am fairly certain that not all of my Vikingars will wish to journey to the Wenro village. For every man you provide to guide me, I will give you a man to replace him on the rowing bench. Even though you won't be sailing to Normandy, you're going to Scandinavia, so my men will be closer to home."

"Agreed," they said as they clasped wrists.

Magnus left the longhouse and found Baldr and Fólki and told them of the arrangement with Ketill. Magnus explained that any of their crewmen, whom the captains felt they could spare, were welcome to accompany Ketill back to the Wenro village. Baldr and Fólki departed to talk to their crews, and Magnus called his own drakkar crew together. After gathering his crewmen, Magnus told them, "The two karvi ships anchored out in the bay are going to journey to the Wenro village we just left. I warned them to be wary of the Iroquois Skraelings on the same lake. I told Ketill, their captain, that it would be wise to take one of you along as a guide to show them safely to the Wenro. No one will be ordered to do this; it will be strictly volunteer. Understand that we won't wait here for you. I have no idea when Ketill will return to Vinland, so if you join his Viking now, you'll be a part of it until it returns to Normandy. I will leave you all to make your own decisions. If you do want to join Ketill, come find me."

At that point Magnus departed to find Baldr and Fólki and ask them if their ships were ready for the trans-ocean passage. Magnus found that Balder had Håkon repairing some iron rivets on his skeid, while his crew was using caulking consisting of either tarred wool or animal fur to make the ship watertight.

Seeing that Baldr was on top of things, Magnus approached Fólki and saw that his men were also using caulking procured from the Vinlanders to caulk the ship. He also noticed that the ships carpenter was using a twist drill bit, to drill holes for treenails on a new plank for the hull. The original plank had split open at some point, and while the crew had been able to caulk the hole adequately for lake sailing, they were not going to trust that for sailing in the north Atlantic.

Magnus had also tasked his crew to perform upkeep on his long-ship and went to check on it. As he approached his drakkar, he noticed men replacing the caulking and sewing a tear in the sail. When he saw four men standing by the dragonhead prow and intently looking up at it, he was curious as to what they were doing and approached them.

"Is the dragon whispering words of wisdom to you?"

The men laughed and one of them answered, "No Jarl, we have a request."

"From me or the dragon?"

The men laughed again. "Both Jarl."

Now thoroughly interested, Magnus motioned the men to speak. One of them said, "Forungi, when we were with the Erie, I was given these beautiful pieces of rock."

The man held out two pieces of red quartz that had been nicely polished by the Skraelings. Magnus admired the rose-colored rocks and stated,

"Those are good looking rocks, but what have they to do with our dragon?"

"Jarl, we would like your permission to hammer these into the dragon's eyes." Looking from the quartz to the dragonhead prow of his ship, Magnus said, "Every dragon should have blood red eyes, so hammer away!"

Magnus was approached by Fólki. "Jarl, I spoke to my crew, and I have one man who desires to go with Ketill." "Can you spare him?"

"I can spare him. Once this fellow heard about Baldr's man remaining behind, he was kicking himself for not asking the same, as he left a Wenro girlfriend behind as well."

Magnus found the same thing was true on his ship; one man wanted to go with Ketill because of a Wenro maiden. Later Baldr told him that all his were ready to return home to the Vik.

Magnus went to find Ketill who was overseeing the final loading procedures of his ships. Magnus walked up to him and said, "I have procured you two guides to lead you to the Wenro village. They are both good Vikingars that will serve you well."

"Thank you kindly, Jarl. I said that I would ask my crew for anyone wishing to return to Scandinavia to replace your men. After hearing your men's tales of the Wenro village, all want to see that for themselves, and perhaps get some valuable beaver pelts! Nevertheless, I am a man of my word, and since I can't find volunteers, I will pick two for you."

"No need for that. I still have more crewman than rowing benches, so take your entire crew and go visit my Wenro friends."

Later, Magnus spoke to Håkon at his iron smithy in the village. "Have you missed your old workshop?"

"Not the work so much, as I did plenty of that with the Erie, but I have missed having a proper foundry."

"That brings me to my next question. Do you wish to remain here or accompany us back to Norseland?"

"What I truly enjoy doing is blacksmithing, and that is what I can do here. If I return to Norseland, I will have to find a foundry that needs a smith, and I don't know how long that'll take. Here, I can go back to blacksmithing immediately. So, I will remain."

"I thought as much. As a token of my appreciation of your invaluable services, I will leave you five beaver pelts." Håkon drew to his full height and stated, "It has been an honor Jarl; I wish you fair winds and following seas back to Norseland."

Chapter Fourteen

The repairs on the three ships were complete, and the captains deemed them each seaworthy. The final supplies were procured from the Vinland merchants, and the village Hetman had a goodbye celebration for Magnus and his captains. This Viking had brought a considerable amount of commerce to the village, and the Hetman was eager for their return.

Next morning, Magnus's Viking pushed off from the Vinland beaches and began their journey back across the ocean. The plan was for them to sail roughly eight hundred miles north to the settlement at Eiriksfjord, Greenland. Once there, they would resupply with freshwater and any other items running low. They would sail in an easterly heading for approximately another eight hundred miles to reach the Viking colony of Iceland. So long as they didn't encounter stormy weather that would blow them far off course, each leg of their journey shouldn't take more than a handful of days each.

Their sail to first Greenland and then to Iceland was uneventful. Once they arrived in Iceland, they began re-provisioning the ships, and Magnus took time to gather news about events in Norseland. He did this out of more than idle curiosity. In recent years, several kings were growing in power throughout the Viking lands, and as they gained power, they absorbed neighboring kingdoms and established dynasties. It was obvious to Magnus that the days of the relatively independent Viking earldoms, fiefdoms, and petty kingdoms were numbered, and soon a handful of powerful kings would rule all of Scandinavia. That could have come much closer to reality since he sailed away from home.

Many decades prior, King Harald Fairhair had done much to unify Norseland into one entity. After Harald died, his two sons, Eric Bloodaxe and Haakon the Good, inherited their father's kingdom. After their deaths, the unification of Norseland died as well. But in recent years multiple civil wars were fought. Magnus knew that the only way these conflicts would end was the appointment of a king who would introduce a clear law of succession. There had been much talk of late that King Håkonsson would be the man to make that happen, but that remained to be seen.

Magnus spent the day listening to local gossip while his men prepared the vessels. Their sailing route would take them by the Viking colonies in the Faroe Islands, but Magnus had no intention of stopping, unless they needed to. By days end, Magnus had listened to all the gossip he cared to over several cups of mead at a local watering hole. Magnus told his captains to let their men hit the local taverns after the ship's preparations were complete.

Iceland was in many ways a small Norseland, so it felt like being home. Although they were in a Viking colony, and in no danger, all three ships posted security throughout the night. The Icelanders had learned of the ships' valuable cargo of beaver pelts, and if left unattended, the pelts would vanish.

The next morning dawned clear and bright, and Magnus's drakkar and skeids rowed out of the busy harbor. Once clear, they shipped their oars and raised their sails. The wind was still favorable, and all indications were that Njord, the god of the sea and seafarers, was still smiling on their Viking.

By early afternoon, clouds had set in and a gentle, yet steady rain had begun to fall. This was in no way one of the infamous North Atlantic storms that usually occurred in the winter and were accompanied by gale force winds. Nevertheless, the sun was completely obscured by the cloudbank. As Viking ships required a bearing of the sun to navigate by, if they couldn't see it, they used one of their most valuable tools, the sunstone, which Magnus was an expert at using. Based on his observations, Magnus estimated that they had drifted slightly north of their intended direction of travel. Therefore, he told his ship's helmsman to adjust their route of sail to compensate. As Magnus's drakkar was in the lead, the other two ships would follow in trace.

As the day turned to evening, the clouds persisted. Magnus took out his sunstone one final time, and saw that they now had drifted slightly south, so once again he had the helmsman adjust course. This was the final sighting he would take tonight, and if it remained cloudy all night, he wouldn't be able to adjust their course again till dawn.

He hoped the clouds would pass over sometime that night, revealing the moon and stars. If a mariner could see the constellation of the god Odin's Wagon, he knew exactly where north was. As their route of sail was easterly, all Magnus had to do was keep Odin's Wagon to the port side of their vessel, and east they would go. After taking the final sunstone reading, Magnus turned in for the night on a mattress made of multiple beaver pelts, which like the other captains, he kept close by to keep them safe.

He slept soundly, as he almost always did at sea, and was awoken at dawn by the ship's lookout shouting of "Sail Ho." He jumped up to see who had been sighted. The sky had cleared, and then quickly he spotted three cogs sailing on a route perpendicular to them. The cog was a type of square-rigged merchantman equipped with a rudder at the stern. These were large ships and almost certainly carrying cargo.

As Vikingars were certainly willing to plunder ships at sea, Magnus decided to intercept them and see what they had aboard. He ordered one of his crew to climb the mast and raise the raven flag, the signal to prepare to board the sighted vessels.

Magnus adjusted course to intercept the first ship, and Baldr and Fólki sailed for the other two. It didn't take long for the merchant ships to turn away to remain as far from the drakkar and skeids as possible. They shouldn't have bothered.

The cogs were fitted with a single mast and a square-rigged single sail. The three ranged from about fifty to eighty feet in length with a beam of fifteen to twenty-five feet. Magnus estimated that the one he was approaching could carry hundreds of tons of cargo. These were cargo ships, not war ships, so they weren't nearly as fast or maneuverable, and they didn't have multiple benches of oarsmen.

The Viking ships would have overtaken the ships without the men rowing, but Magnus had them do so anyway, to get their blood pumping in preparation for a possible fight.

As Magnus's drakkar with the dragon head prow bearing red quartz eyes came alongside the lead cog, the merchant captain accepted the inevitable and dropped sail. As they came abreast, three of Magnus's men threw grappling hooks over the cog's railing to affix the two ships together. His men lined their vessel's side, helmets on and swords in hand, ready to swarm aboard the other ship.

Magnus looked across at the other ship's deck and saw no more than ten men, none of them armed. These sailors certainly understood that resistance was futile and were meekly awaiting their fate. Seeing this, Magnus motioned for his men to remain in place as he and three others boarded the cog.

Magnus was first greeted by a man who was wearing a crucifix and speaking in Latin. From his Jomsviking service in Sicily, Magnus recognized this man as a Christian priest, and that these vessels were likely from the Mediterranean or Iberian Peninsula.

After the man finished making the Sign of the Cross, Magnus said, "I don't suppose any of you speak my language?" To his surprise, the man who Magnus assumed was the ship's captain replied," Aye, I speak a bit of Norse."

"What is your name and where do you come from?"

"My name is Lorencio Didacus, and we sailed from Galicia in Spain, by way of Dublin, in the land of the Gaels." Dublin was a Viking settlement in what the Gaels called Ireland. Much of Ireland had been taken over by the Vikings hundreds of years before. They had largely been driven out by the Gaels under King Brian Boru several decades ago, but over the last few years had returned to reestablish control over their colony of Dublin. The Vikings had intermarried with the local Irish, and their descendants were now known as the Norse-Gaels.

Dublin was one of the most important mercantile centers in the Viking world, so it was understandable why Lorencio would be going there, and why he was somewhat fluent in the Norse language.

"What is your cargo?" Fully understanding the reason Magnus asked that question, Lorencio's face fell as he answered, "Copper ingots mined by the Gaels."

Conversely, Magnus's face lit up on hearing this information. While copper wasn't nearly as valuable as precious metals like gold or silver, it was still very much in demand throughout Europe. In the recent past, there had been an increase in the use of copper and its alloys for making everyday objects. Candlesticks, dress accessories such as sequins, and belt buckles were now commonly made of copper. Additionally, domestic vessels such as cauldrons, skillets, basins and other pots and pans for the kitchen or dining table were copper.

It was sought after for hand-crafted products such as boilers for baths, weighing scales and other measuring instruments. Furthermore, the growing Christian church was using copper for items manufactured for liturgical use. Made-to-order copper Church accessories included candelabra, pulpits, baptisteries, fountains, funeral monuments, and bells. Finally, copper was a primary component of the main alloys used in the coinage of most Kingdoms.

The result of this piracy-at-sea would be that Magnus's Viking would procure numerous and highly marketable items. Magnus had his men board the vessel and start carrying the copper ingots aboard his ship. The ingots of reddish metal were shaped somewhat like a bun and weighed between five and ten pounds each. The Spanish vessel contained several hundred ingots, but Magnus's men worked vigorously to remove them. Magnus could see that Baldr and Fólki were doing the same on the vessels they had boarded.

As his men plundered the copper ingots, one of Magnus's senior Vikingars approached him. "Jarl, I noticed that the crucifix on that holy man appears to be gold; are you intending on taking it, or may I?" Magnus had noticed it earlier and in his younger days would have ripped it off the priest's neck immediately. Since the acquisition of his thrall Brigid, the former nun, he had begun to feel differently. She had spent considerable time telling Magnus and his wife Esja about her religion, and Brigid had even made a crucifix to hang on the wall above where she slept in their longhouse. If Magnus allowed his man to rob the priest of his crucifix, he realized that he would feel something akin to shame.

"I think not. Let the holy man keep his cross, and we will satisfy ourselves with these thousands of pounds of copper." As his men were finishing loading the last of the copper and throwing overboard many of the rocks they had been using for ballast in the long-ship, Baldr and Fólki's ships rowed alongside the cog. Once abreast, both men boarded the cog and approached Magnus.

Fólki said, "Jarl, what do you think about putting prize crews from each of our ships aboard the cogs and sailing them back to the Vik? Once there, we can sell the cogs to merchants. We can also sell off the crews at a thrall auction."

Magnus considered it. "If we do, we will have to find places to hold thirty thralls until they can be sold. We are all very much looking forward to seeing our loved ones upon our return. Having to watch after imprisoned slaves isn't something any of us will want to do. We have hundreds of beaver pelts worth their weight in gold, we now have thousands of copper ingots worth a great amount. We will let the three cogs go, so we can plunder them again later."

Having their answer, Fólki and Baldr boarded their ships and prepared to make sail.

As Magnus prepared to cross over to his drakkar, Lorencio said, "Jarl, I would like to thank you for not killing us, nor taking us to be enthralled."

"If you had offered us resistance, you and your men surely would have died. If we decided to enslave you all, we would have to watch you until sold. We are returning from a long Viking beyond Vinland and are just ready to be home with our families. Consider yourselves lucky."

"I believe that Christos interceded with you to spare our lives and our freedom."

Magnus turned away to board his own ship. "He may have; he very well may have."

Chapter Fifteen

The rest of the journey to the Vik passed uneventfully. There was another day of overcast and rain, but no heavy wind. The sunstones did their job indicating direction, and shortly afterward they saw the coastline and could pilot using that. They three longships pulled into their home port and tied up to the pier.

They had been gone for more than a year and were thought to be lost. As soon they were sighted, word spread like fire. By the time they docked, the waterfront was full of friends and family with more appearing by the minute. As Magnus's farmstead was several miles away from the fjord, he knew it would be a while before Esja arrived.

Magnus spent the time with Fólki and Baldr passing out the accumulated spoils to their Vikingars. Each man approached the captain's quarters, where he was handed two or more pelts each. Magnus, Baldr and Fólki had each developed their own unique formulas for pelt apportionment, based on each man's contributions to the Viking. Regardless of how many pelts each man received, knowing their value, they were all thrilled.

After passing out all the pelts, the captains then turned to the copper ingots. Each ship had approximately a ton of ingots on board, and each captain set aside a couple dozen for himself. This resulted in there being enough ingots for each Vikingar to get several, depending on how the Captains allocated them. These could all be sold to local metalsmiths for a good price. As Magnus's Skald Dómaldr, was retrieving his ingots, Magnus asked him, "When will you finish my saga?"

"Jarl, I need to transcribe the individual chapters I wrote, many on deerskin, onto one complete parchment. This will probably take me at least a week or more, and then I will bring it to your longhouse to read it to you."

"Very well. I will have the mead ready for us when you arrive." As Magnus was looking at his preserved beaver musk sacs, wondering how best to sell them, he heard Esja calling his name.

He looked up and saw his wife, accompanied by Brigid, waving to him as they ran to the ship. Taking Esja in his arms and kissing her, he noticed that her nose had been recently broken and was still swollen and bruised.

Still holding her, Magnus asked, "Did one of our cows kick you in the face?"

"Nothing so domestic as that, come along home and I will tell you all about it." Magnus loaded all his possessions into the Ox cart that Esja and Brigid arrived in. The women were both astounded at his multiple beaver pelts and Esja couldn't help but run her fingers through the fur.

Magnus told Esja, "Select two of the most beautiful pelts for yourself and pick one for Brigid as well. Those should keep you both warm in the winter.

As Brigid held the reins of the oxen, Esja asked Magnus all about the Viking. Magnus recounted everything from start to finish, talking the whole hour it took them to reach the farmstead. Magnus hadn't talked so much in his entire life and was exhausted upon arrival home.

The other thralls came out of the barn upon their return, and helped Brigid unhitch the oxen and carry all the ingots into the barn. Magnus and Esja carried his gear and pelts into the longhouse. As they walked in and put everything down, Magnus asked, "Now, what walloped your face?"

Esja headed out the door saying, "I'll be right back."

She returned a moment later. "I told Brigid to remain with the other thralls until I call her. And I will tell you about my injury after I welcome my husband home appropriately."

With that, Esja slipped out of her dress and then she and Magnus made love in such a manner that all their thralls could hear from outside.

After making love and catching their breath, Magnus got up out of bed and poured them both some mead. Returning to bed, Magnus asked, "All right, gorgeous, so how did you injure your face, and does it still hurt?"

"My nose was broken several weeks ago, and the village Seiðr had to set it, but I think that she did well."

Magnus gently ran his finger along Esja's nose. "She did. It's straight, and there is barely a bump, and that will probably go down as the bruising fades. How did it happen? You and Brigid didn't get drunk on mead and get in a brawl, did you?"

"No, but Brigid does factor in the tale."

Now thoroughly curious, Magnus eagerly awaited the story.

"It is very good that you gave us extensive shieldmaiden training before you left."

Magnus's heart sank as he understood what she meant by her comment. "What happened?"

Esja took a deep breath. "A month past from this coming Friday, we were all working here on the farm when a young lad from down the fjord ran up. Out of breath and panting, he told us a longship had raided the village down the coast and was on its way here. I sent Brigid and the other thralls throughout the area, spreading the alarm. While they were out doing so, I grabbed my shield and weapons, and went to the designated assembly area to await the others.

As they arrived, I formed them into the ranks we practiced so many times. Some shieldmaidens never came, but enough did that we were to form the lines. While waiting, we rehearsed the battle drills yet again."

"Why did some shieldmaidens not muster?"

"All were willing, but one was bed-ridden with the measles; one's teeth were so infected and her fever so high that she could barely stand. Two more were pregnant. And during our monthly training, I told the girls that if we were attacked, I wanted no women carrying a child to fight. I refused to be responsible if a pregnant woman was slain, along with her unborn child."

"A well thought out plan, which I would expect from you, which is why I picked you as the leader of shieldmaidens."

"I sent two thralls to watch the shoreline and warn us as soon as they saw the long-ship. The other thralls I sent to help the elderly and young load their valuables in carts to move further up the valley. I kept Brigid next to me in the shield wall."

"After a wait, the two thralls on sentry duty ran up and said that the longship with approximately fifty Vikingars was making land. We then left the longhouse and took up position to await them."

"Where did you position yourselves?"

"Exactly where you told us to, on the hilltop leading into the village."

"Excellent! And why?"

"Because that position forces the attackers to assault uphill, against gravity."

"Why is that important?"

"It causes the attackers to lose momentum. We were formed and ready for them when they came."

They stopped at the bottom of the hill and sent an emissary. He was a young lad in his teens and spoke with a Danish accent. He said that they only came to take any valuables, and if we lay down our shields and weapons, he promised us we wouldn't be harmed, raped, or enthralled."

"I hope you didn't believe any of that gibberish?!"

"I told him that if they wanted our valuables, to come and take them. We then turned around, bent over, and lifted our skirts, showing him our naked bums"

"I only wish I could have been here to see that!"

"The boy turned around and ran back to the group. Knowing what was coming next, we tightened our shield wall, drew our weapons, and sang songs to calm our nerves."

"Brigid said a Christian prayer asking God to protect us in the upcoming battle. The raiding Vikingars tried but really couldn't form a Svinfylking, because of the longhouses on either side of them. Instead, those with bows shot arrows at us."

"Any casualties?" "We held our shields up at the angle you taught us, and on the first volley, the arrows pierced nothing but wood. Seeing it had no effect, they fired one more volley; other than one arrow penetrating the foot of a shieldmaiden, that had the same effect."

"After that, a Vikingar that I assume was their leader, asked us again to lay down our arms. To which we responded with invectives about their lack of manhood, and why were they afraid to attack women?

He didn't like that so next those with spears hurled them."

Taking a sip of his mead, Magnus asked, "Did their spears have more effect than their arrows?"

Shaking her head, Esja replied, "The only difference was we felt it more when they hit our shields. One spear point did penetrate one of the shields and went into the shieldmadin's forearm about an inch. We pulled the spear out, and as it hadn't penetrated an artery, we bandaged it up and she stayed in the fight."

"After they saw that their projectile weapons were having little effect on us, they decided to attack us in hand-to-hand combat."

As Magnus refilled their cups of mead, Esja continued, "As you taught us, their having to come at us up-hill limited the effect of their charge, and the narrowness of the street prevented them from forming a true Svinfylking. I'm certain the impact against our shield wall was much less than they hoped for."

"Certainly so."

"I was positioned at the center of our wall, with Brigid on my right. Our wall was two ranks deep, with either end anchored to a house on either side of the street. Because of the narrow street, they could only come at us about a dozen abreast.

"We caught their shields on ours, and they started swinging their swords and axes attempting to break our wall. As you said in training, many came at us with their arms above their heads positioning their weapons for a powerful downward slash. After all our practice, we knew what to do, every one of us. We stabbed our spears into their guts before they could close enough to swing."

"The maiden two down on my left, got a clean thrust into a raider's unarmored belly, and when he fell back off the spear point, it opened his stomach and his guts spilled out on the ground. During training, you warned us about that, but training is a lot different. Seeing it with your own eyes, it's shocking. Another maiden in the wall to my right was able to thrust her spear low, into the raider's groin and relieved him of his manhood."

"I hope for his sake he already had children, as he certainly won't have anymore."

After draining the rest of her flagon of mead, Esja continued. "The raiders broke off at that point and retreated down the hill. The gelded Vikingar was able to limp behind his comrades, trailing blood. The one that had been eviscerated lay on his back with his guts piled besides him, shrieking in pain. After listening to him for several minutes, several of the maidens wondered aloud how long before he died."

"When I was a Jomsviking, one of our leaders was disemboweled in a battle. We won the fight but decided not to leave the battlefield until our leader had died. It took several, excruciating hours."

"I remembered you telling me about that after one of your nightmares. And now I understand a little about why you have those nightmares."

Magnus stared off into the distance. "The battles usually last only a short time, but they remain in your head much, much longer."

"We listened to the man wail for several minutes until I could no longer bear it. The raiders were still down the hill, so I left the shield wall and walked to him. He was begging me in a heavy Danish accent to put him out of his misery, so I took my spear and did so."

Esja shivered as she said that. He put his arms around her and held her.

"I sometimes think about him and wonder if he had a wife that loved him, and if he had children, that would never see their father again."

Still holding her Magnus softly said, "He and his comrades were attempting to loot our village, and in the process kill or wound you shieldmaidens. And if they had succeeded in breaking the shield wall, you know exactly what they would have done to all surviving shieldmaidens."

Wiping a tear from her eye, Esja composed herself and added, "I know, but that was the first man I've killed. And while I know that it was their choice to attack us, and that we were defending ourselves, our families, and our homes, I still didn't like it. I don't want to do it ever again."

Magnus kissed her forehead. "I hope and pray that you'll never have to."

After refilling their flagons of mead, Esja went on, "The raiders had now developed a new plan of attack, and they started advancing at us again. About half-way up the hill, many of them in the rear of their formation left the street and went into the alleys on either side. We realized what they were doing, and I had the second rank of shieldmaidens face about. Sure enough, those Vikingars then reformed behind us, and we were attacked from both directions."

Magnus sipped his mead as he waited for her to continue. "After the damage we did with our spears during their first attack, they adjusted their tactics. Instead of coming at us with their swords and axes raised above their heads, they came at us with their shields lowered to take our spear points. This tactic was much more effective. We thrust our spears at them once they were within range, but most hit their shields. If one of our spear points got stuck in the shield wood, the Vikingars would then swing their sword or axe at our spear, cutting it in two. Then the maidens would have to drop their useless spear hafts and draw their swords. That was exactly what happened to me.

"A big Dane, almost as tall as you, came at me with his shield lowered."

Magnus interrupted her at this point, "While I'm thinking of it, what colors and designs were painted on their shields?"

"As you looked at the shields, most had the left side painted green, and the right side yellow. And they had a black raven painted in the middle."

If Magnus decided on a retribution raid on the assailants, he now had useful information by which to locate them in Denmark.

"This giant kept his shield low. He cut my spear in half with his axe. I dropped it and yanked out my sword. While I was doing that, he raised his Sparth axe up and delivered a mighty downward swing at my shield. He swung with such might that his blow drove the rim of my shield into my face. It struck me on the bridge of the nose, just under the iron helmet. The impact was such that it knocked me senseless and I fell on my back helpless. I have no recollection of what happened next, but the other maidens said the giant stood over me with axe raised to cleave me in two. Seeing what was happening, Brigid dropped her spear and shield and threw herself on top of me to screen me from his blow. This unexpected occurrence momentarily distracted the Dane who just stood over us with his axe raised. Before he could swing it down on us, Hilda, who was on the other side of me, thrust her spear deep into the Dane's unprotected armpit. It must have hit a vital organ, as he dropped mortally wounded."

"We think that he must have been their leader, because when all the other Vikingars saw him fall, they lost heart and retreated down to their drakkar. I was revived after several minutes and told about of this."

Magnus sat in stunned silence for several moments absorbing all this. "Were there any other wounds amongst the shieldmaidens, besides the one who took an arrow in the foot and the one a spear in the arm?"

Esja solemnly nodded her head. "Aye, Vor was slashed across the arm with a sword. It didn't sever it, but it has since become infected and the pus is running. She is weak but was still alive, as of two days ago. Borghild was struck with an axe on the head and it killed her outright. Heidrun caught a sword blow that hit her right collar bone. It crushed the bone and bit deep into her upper chest. She lingered for a couple of days and then died. There were a few more with bruises and minor cuts, but nothing else significant."

"After the maidens were sure that the Danes had departed, they broke the shield wall and fetched the village Seiðr, who had remained behind when the other villagers left. She tended to all the wounded and set my nose. Afterwards, one of the maidens rode up the glen to let everyone know it was safe to return."

Magnus gave Esja a lengthy hug. "If Brigid hadn't stopped that Dane from cleaving you with his axe, Odin's Valkyries would have taken you to Valhalla, since you would have died in battle. You may have enjoyed Odin's hall, but I would have missed you terribly. So, I'm glad that they didn't take you."

As they embraced, Esja said, "I would not be holding you now if not for Brigid. I wish to talk about her."

Chapter Sixteen

Magnus looked at Esja. "She willingly risked her life to save yours. As of this moment, she is no longer a thrall and is free. I will make a public announcement of this fact at the next Thing."

"I would have been very upset if you didn't agree to it."

"Happy wife, happy life!"

Esja smiled coyly and ran her fingers down Magnus's face as she replied, "Indeed!" She gazed at him intently and said, "That brings up something else I wish to speak of concerning her. After she is free, there are many men who will wish to marry her."

"Starting with all of my drakkar crew!" He couldn't miss seeing the questioning look in Esja's eyes. "During the Viking, several of my crew approached me about "my beautiful Gaelic thrall" and inquired if I would be willing to sell her to them to become their concubine." I of course dashed their hopes, and I heard rumors that most of my men were convinced that I wouldn't sell her because she was my frille."

"After I was told what she had done for me, I asked her why a thrall would risk her life for her mistress. She replied with a verse from her holy book. I still remember what she said, 'John 15:13 Greater love hath no man than this, that a man lay down his life for his friends.'

"I asked her if she considered me a friend. She said that even though she was our thrall, we treated her kindly, took good care of her, allowed her to sleep in our longhouse, and that you never forced yourself on her."

As Esja then stood up, Magnus smacked her on the bottom. "The only reason I haven't laid with her is because I can hardly keep up with you."

"Brigid said that because we treat her so much better than any thrall could ever expect that she considers us not only friends, but almost family."

"She is a beautiful girl, inside and out. Some man will be very fortunate to convince her to marry him."

Looking over the rim of her flagon, Esja said, "What about you asking her?"

"What?"

"After hearing how she felt about us, I realized that I almost felt like she was my sister, not my thrall. I know that now she is free, it won't be long before some lucky man will marry her and take her Odin knows where. When that happens, I will lose a friend and sister. I don't want that to happen, so I think that you should wed her."

Magnus still stared at her but didn't know what to say, so he said nothing.

Seeing that she had to dumb it down significantly to get through to her husband, Esja went on. "Ever since we married, I've realized that your nearly insatiable sexual appetite would eventually cause you to take another wife. You're a wealthy Vikingar and can afford as many wives as you want. I don't particularly relish the thought of you laying with another woman, but I understand that it is an eventuality. If you take another wife, she will have to share the longhouse with me. I don't know how I'd get along with this woman. Possibly well, but likely not at all.

If it's the latter, then all our existences will be miserable. And even though you'd now have two wives to bed, the dysfunctional home life would probably lead you to go on a Viking at every possible opportunity. I know that I like Brigid; she already lives in our house, so she knows how things work. And as a bonus, since we're essentially the only family she's got here, you won't have to pay a bride price to marry her."

At last, Magnus started coming to full terms with what she was suggesting. "And you're willing to share me sexually with Brigid?"

"I'm sure I will be a little jealous at first, so I will probably go milk a cow or goat in the barn when you two are love making."

"Brigid is a free woman now; she might not accept my marriage proposal."

"Oh, don't worry about that! You were on your Viking for over a year, and she and I had lots of time to talk. Remember, she was a nun and is a virgin, so she has no knowledge of physical love. And as we got closer during your Viking, she felt that she could ask me many things about you and my love making. I would tell her the truth, and the poor girl would be so overcome by lust, I worried that she might faint."

"One morning she approached me and asked me not to tell her anymore about our love making, as she was having torrid dreams about you. I heard her moaning in her sleep, so I now knew what was bothering her! So, yes, I feel very confident that she will indeed accept your proposal."

Magnus stood and said, "Well, if you'll excuse me, I have a thrall to free and propose marriage to."

Esja brought Brigid from the barn to the longhouse and sat her down next to Magnus. He smiled at her and said, "Esja told me how you were willing to sacrifice your life for her in the Danish attack on the village. That was incredibly brave and selfless. Therefore, I am granting you your freedom and will announce it publicly at the next Thing. You are now a free woman and can go wherever you wish. Do you understand what I am saying?"

He stopped to let it sink in.

Finally, she spoke, but the stunned look on her face said all that needed saying. "Jarl, I don't know what to say, other than thank you."

Still trying to get her mind around her new station in life, she said, "Do you want me to leave today, or may I have a few days to figure out where to go next?"

Magnus shook his head. "You don't have to leave today, or ever, if you choose not to."

A thoroughly confused Brigid sat open mouthed looking from Magnus to Esja. Seeing her confusion, Magnus grasped her hand and said, "Brigid, you won't have to leave here as I'm asking you to marry me and become my second wife."

Blushing so red that her skin nearly matched her hair, Brigid didn't respond and just kept looking from Magnus to Esja with her mouth agape.

Seeing the poor girl's distress, Esja said, "Brigid, it is all right, I'm the one who suggested this to Magnus. Over the time that we have owned you, you have become as close as a sister to me. And in that fight last month, you were willing to lay down your life for me. I know that as a free woman, men will be lining up to propose to you. You will eventually marry one of them, and then you would leave. I might never see you again. If you agree to wed Magnus, you will stay here and officially be part of our family. I much prefer that to you leaving us."

Still blushing beet red, Brigid looked at the ground and said, "Mistress, will you allow me and the Jarl to be truly married, and do things that husbands, and wives do?"

"First of all, there is no more Mistress and Master, you are now a free woman. You make your own choices. If I didn't allow you and Magnus to have marital relations, he wouldn't have agreed to ask you to marry him. You will now be able to live your dream that you told me about."

Brigid covered her face with her hands, seeming at a loss for words.

After a long silence, Magnus said, "Brigid, do not feel that you must accept my proposal, if you don't, you can still stay here as long as needed to determine your next move. Only agree to marry me if you truly desire it."

Dropping her hands from her face, Brigid said, "If I agree, will it be all right if we are wed in a Christian ceremony?"

"Absolutely. I know that there is a Christian Priest over in the adjacent Earldom. I will ask him to marry us."

With her face as bright red as humanly possible, Brigid then stood up and answered, "Then the answer is yes!"

The three then all participated in a group hug before Esja and Brigid prepared a celebratory feast. After eating, Magnus said to them both, "If you can gather all the shieldmaidens together, I have something I wish to give them."

Brigid and the thralls then went to tell the maidens to meet at the longhouse the next morning. Magnus also had them ask the deceased shieldmaidens' families to send a representative.

The next morning the twenty-one surviving shieldmaidens gathered at the longhouse. Vor, the one who had received the arm wound which had become infected, had died the previous day. Her father, along with the fathers of the other two deceased maidens attended in their places.

After they were all gathered, Magnus said, "I know each of you from the training we conducted last year. I knew that all of you are brave and strong and were willing to fight to defend your homes and families. And, so you did!

"The marauding Danes had the misfortune to attack a village that was prepared for them. As a result, in addition to your fallen comrades, there are now several Danish Vikingars supping in Valhalla." Motioning them all to gather around him, he reached down and brought-out several copper ingots. He walked down the ranks of the shieldmaidens and gave each one multiple ingots. To the fathers of the slain maidens, he gave several as well.

After passing them out, he said, "These copper ingots were mined on the island of the Gaels. You can take them to any metalsmith or craftsman, and he will pay you handsomely for each. You all served my wife, your families, and this village well. Word will spread throughout Scandinavia about your martial feats, and I doubt our village will be attacked again. If it is, you are all now veterans of battle, and will know exactly what to do." After grasping each woman's wrist as a sign of respect, Magnus dismissed them to return home with their ingots.

He had Esja and Brigid remain with him for a moment. "I know I already gave you both beaver pelts to wear in the winter. Brigid, I only gave you one, as you were my thrall then, not my soon to be wife. So, as an early wedding gift, pick another one."

As Brigid dug through the pelts, Magnus took out his deerskin of beaver musk sacs. Holding one aloft, he explained to the ladies what they were for. Both were as incredulous as he had initially been back in Vinland about their erogenous properties. Rubbing the musk sac between his fingers to activate it, as he'd seen the Skraeling maidens do, he reached first to Esja, and then Brigid rubbing it on their necks beneath their ears. After rubbing it in, he leaned forward to first one then the other to smell his handiwork. After breathing deeply, he motioned for the girls to smell each other's necks. After inhaling the scent, he asked both girls what they thought?"

Esja said, "I now understand why the Skraeling women wear this. For some reason, the scent is very sensual." Wrapping his arm around Esja's waist, Magnus looked at Brigid and asked, "My soon to be second wife, what think you?"

With a bemused look on her face, Brigid answered, "That musk makes me think that you and I should say our vows sooner, rather than later!"

Laughing as he squeezed Esja's bottom, Magnus stated, "I agree wholeheartedly, now if you'll excuse us, my first wife and I need to take care of some things."

As Magnus and Esja walked back to their sleeping quarters, Brigid did all she could to clear her mind of the tempting thoughts that unwed women shouldn't yet have.

As he'd promised, Magnus sent word to the nearby Christian priest, who was called Paul, that he wished him to officiate at the wedding ceremony of Magnus and Brigid. Knowing that Magnus was a wealthy Vikingar that would certainly give a handsome tithe for performing the ceremony, Paul agreed to see Magnus.

Paul asked several questions about Magnus and Brigid. When Paul learned that Brigid had been a nun in Ireland before she was enthralled, he told Magnus that he would need to ask Brigid if she desired to officially leave the cloistered life of a nun. Paul also stated that if she told him that she did want to formally leave the nun-hood, he would need to get permission from the Bishop of local the diocese for it to be official.

To Magnus, this seemed like a lot of trouble for nothing, but he agreed.

Paul then asked if Magnus already had a wife.

Magnus said, "Yes, Brigid will be my second wife. Is that a problem?"

"Several years ago, Norse Bishop Øystein Erlendsson declared that concubines were not allowed to accept the Christian sacraments unless they married. The Bishop also stated that men should be forced to promise marriage to women they had lain with outside of wedlock. The Bishop did not say that a man having multiple wives was prohibited under scripture, so you are allowed to marry Brigid, after the diocese gives its approval. Of course, for me to do the wedding, you will need to convert to Christianity."

Brigid had told Magnus of this requirement, and he had thought about it. He knew that Christianity was the growing religion in the Viking lands. And he thought of all he had been taught over his lifetime about the Norse Gods. Their incessant fighting with each other, lying to each other, tricking each other, etc. And it dawned on him that the gods all seemed to behave so much like men. He then thought about what Brigid said that the Bible taught about Jesus, the only son of God, being crucified to offer salvation to mankind. When Magnus asked what crucifixion was, Brigid explained that it was the Roman version of a Blood Eagle.

When Magnus asked her why the son of God would allow himself to die horribly, Brigid said, "So that all of us unworthy humans could go to heaven when we die."

"Was your Jesus' willingness to die, the reason you were willing to do the same for Esja?"

Brigid lowered her eyes and said, "I felt that following Christ's example was the right thing to do."

"Then your Jesus will be my Jesus as well." Recounting that news to Paul, Paul responded by saying, "Excellent, we will conduct the official conversion process and your baptism while we await the diocese approval of Brigid's removal from her role as a nun."

Over the next several weeks, Magnus learned the beliefs of the Christian religion while he and Paul awaited the bishop's approval of the former nun's marriage. Finally, they received word that they were to come to the church where Bishop Eirik officiated.

Once there the bishop informed them that the diocese had authorized Brigid to marry. Bishop Eirik asked Paul if Magnus was ready for his confirmation. Paul stated he was and told Magnus to prepare for the ritual of Confirmation. Magnus kneeled before the bishop. Paul, acting as Magnus's sponsor, laid one hand on your shoulder and spoke his confirmation name. Magnus's chosen confirmation name was suggested by Brigid. She told him that the Archangel St. Michael is the patron saint of the warrior. She said that she couldn't imagine a more appropriate name for him, and he agreed. The bishop then anointed Magnus by using consecrated oil and making the Sign of the Cross on his forehead while saying Magnus's Confirmation name.

The Bishop continued by saying, "Be sealed with the gift of the Holy Spirit' in Latin. Magnus responded, "Amen." The bishop finished with, "Peace be with you."

And so, Magnus was officially a Christian and able to marry Brigid.

Chapter Seventeen

Norse wedding ceremonies were involved processes and took significant time and preparation. While Paul would be performing a Christian ceremony, Magnus had asked him if including traditional Norse customs would pose a problem. Paul answered that so long as the wedding customs didn't include the worship of Norse gods, there should be no issues.

Since many wedding customs did involve veneration of one or the other of the multitude of Norse gods, Brigid and Magnus decided to forgo those. Others, such as the traditions of the two drinking from the same cup called the loving-cup, to further symbolize their union, they included.

Magnus asked Paul if the Viking tradition of the bride and groom being required to get drunk on mead, also called bridal ale, would be a problem.

Paul thought before he answered, "Jesus' first miracle included turning water into wine. However, the Bible is also full of warnings against over drinking." After considering it for a moment longer, Paul continued, "Even though you'll both be drunk on bridal ale, you'll be husband and wife, so whatever the two of you do after the ceremony shouldn't be sinful. So, drink up!"

Weddings were traditionally held on a Friday, as that was Freya, or Frigga's day, and Frigga was the goddess of weddings, love, childbirth, and mothers. Father Paul said that as long as the couple didn't worship or make sacrifices to Frigga, getting married on the day dedicated and named after her, was fine.

As Brigid wouldn't have any relatives in attendance, some customs had to be ignored. For example, the custom of a Brullaup, which consisted of relatives of the groom competing in a foot race against relatives of the bride. The losers were then required to serve alcohol to the victors during the wedding wild boar feast.

While that was a fun tradition that Esja and Magnus had at their wedding, after Brigid and Magnus's nuptials, all the guests would have to get their own drinks.

Another Norse wedding tradition they would ignore was that when the banquet was over, the couple would go to bed with as many as six witnesses, who would certify that their marriage was completed. The consecration of their union had to be witnessed so there could be no questioning of the validity of the union. This tradition was more legal than religious, as it solidified the marriage alliance of two families. Brigid didn't have any family in attendance to care, and Magnus doubted that shy Brigid would be willing to have their lovemaking observed by a group either, so they disregarded it outright in their wedding planning.

Magnus and Brigid's wedding were attended by most of the men that had accompanied his Viking. It was an uproarious event that involved much feasting, drinking, and merrymaking. Magnus made sure that his skald, Dómaldr, was in attendance. During the feast, Magnus asked Dómaldr if his saga was ready, and Dómaldr answered that it was. Magnus told Dómaldr to come to his longhouse the following week, and Magnus would share some of his honey-mead with Dómaldr as he read the saga to them all.

The Vikingars that had brought home Skraeling women were in attendance with their wives. Brigid and Esja were introduced to the girls, who had been learning the Norse language over the last several weeks.

While the women were conversing, Baldr and Fólki approached Magnus. "Jarl, have you heard about the trouble in the Southern and Western Isles?" asked Fólki.

"Aye, I've heard tell of some, but what have you heard?" Baldr said, "The Scotti tribe, which came from the island of the Gaels, has settled in the western islands that are under Norse over-lordship. The Gaels and Norse intermarried and have become known as the Norse-Gaels."

"The Scotti tribe has been growing in size and power for several hundred years and the Norse-Gaels are beginning to resent being under a far-away Norse king's control. There has been much talk about them trying to break away and become independent."

"I have heard this too. And I've also heard tell that our Norse King Haakon won't tolerate this and will lead an expedition to bring the Scotti to heel."

Fólki said, "We have heard that Haakon is currently organizing an invasion of the Western Isles and will be requiring each Earldom pledging loyalty to him to provide men and ships.

Shaking his head, Magnus said, "That will surely include our Earldom."

Baldr said, "We both agree that if we are told that we have to go and fight the Scotti, we wish to serve under you."

Grasping each man's wrist in turn, Magnus said, "Since my remote ancestor was the King Magnus that conquered much of the Western Isles, I'm sure that I have distant relatives there now. This would not be a Viking I would choose to go on, but it looks like we may not have a choice. I would be honored to serve with you both."

"Let's talk no more of this on my wedding night and let us go drink some more mead!"

CPSIA information can be obtained
at www.ICGtesting.com
Printed in the USA
LVHW092354190221
679370LV00005B/306

9 781952 439018